MURDER ON AN ITALIAN ISLAND

T. A. WILLIAMS

B

Boldwood

First published in Great Britain in 2025 by Boldwood Books Ltd.

Copyright © T. A. Williams, 2025

Cover Design by JD Design Ltd.

Cover Images: Shutterstock

A CIP catalogue record for this book is available from the British Library.

Paperback ISBN 978-1-83518-802-6

Large Print ISBN 978-1-83518-803-3

Hardback ISBN 978-1-83518-801-9

Ebook ISBN 978-1-83518-804-0

Kindle ISBN 978-1-83518-805-7

Audio CD ISBN 978-1-83518-796-8

MP3 CD ISBN 978-1-83518-797-5

Digital audio download ISBN 978-1-83518-800-2

This book is printed on certified sustainable paper. Boldwood Books is dedicated to putting sustainability at the heart of our business. For more information please visit https://www.boldwoodbooks.com/about-us/sustainability/

Boldwood Books Ltd, 23 Bowerdean Street, London, SW6 3TN

www.boldwoodbooks.com

To Mariangela and Christina, with love as always

1

ONE EVENING IN MAY

All around were the red tiled roofs of the picturesque, medieval town of San Gimignano, but today, the view was marred by the presence of a body stretched out on the flagstones of the little piazza far below. Even from this height, the inspector recognised the silver hair of the pathologist as he and his team set about their work. From up here, at the top of one of the tallest of San Gimignano's dozen or more towers, the tree-clad hills of Tuscany rolled away into the distance on all sides, and it was hard to believe that a violent death could have taken place in such a serene and beautiful setting. Under other circumstances, it would have been one of the best views in Italy, but not today.

By the inspector's side, Sergeant Romolo had no doubt.

'Looks pretty straightforward to me, sir. It's obvious that he jumped. A classic case of suicide, I reckon.'

The inspector didn't reply immediately. He just stood, surveying the scene and trying to make sense of it. Finally, he glanced across at the sergeant and voiced his concerns. 'If it was suicide, I'm at a loss to know why he did it. A shopkeeper from Florence is enjoying a day out in the Tuscan countryside when he suddenly decides to end it all. Why would he do that?'

Romolo shrugged his shoulders. 'Could be anything... Maybe he had money worries, women trouble. Who knows?'

'That's what we have to find out, Romolo, because until we know that, we can't rule out foul play.'

The sergeant gave his boss a sceptical look. 'You think somebody climbed all the way up here to murder this guy? Why do that and, more importantly, why did the victim agree to climb the tower with a potential murderer?'

The inspector added a proviso. 'Who says they climbed the tower together? Maybe the victim climbed up on his own to see the view, and the killer was already here, waiting for him. Alternatively, the killer might have seen him enter the tower and followed him up.' He gave a frustrated sigh. 'Of course, you're right, the obvious conclusion is that he jumped, but there's just something about this that bothers me. It's too easy, somehow.' He caught the young sergeant's eye. 'Just call it a hunch, Romolo. There's something here that doesn't make sense.'

* * *

I sat back and stretched my legs, realising that I'd been sitting here staring at the computer screen for over an hour. The story had been going so well until the beginning of the month – and I was well over halfway through writing the book – but for the last week and a half, I hadn't typed a word. I was stuck. I glanced down at Oscar, who was sprawled on the terracotta tiles at my feet, and turned to him for help.

'I don't suppose you can come up with a solution to writer's block, can you?' I had read about this phenomenon online in various authors' groups, but, in my relatively short writing career up till now, this was the first time I had experienced it so acutely.

He looked up at me but gave no response. In fairness, I didn't really expect one. Oscar is a dog, after all, and as such, he's a good listener, but not a conversationalist.

I sat there and went through the plot again in my head – the robbery, the first murder, the investigation that had led inexorably to San Gimignano and now this extra ramping up of the tension with the discovery of another body. The problem was that I had backed myself into a corner, and I had no idea how to get out of it. Although I'm normally a pretty organised person, my editor in London describes me as a seat-of-the-pants writer and she's right. Rather than plan everything in advance, I tend to select a location, decide on some of the main characters, throw in some jeopardy and see where it all leads. In the case of this book, the answer so far was: nowhere.

I pushed back my chair and glanced back down at Oscar. 'Maybe a walk might be a good idea to clear my head. Interested?'

As always, the magic word did the trick, and he jumped to his feet a lot more agilely than I did – but he is barely four and I'm almost fifty-four years older than him. I reached back and closed the laptop regretfully before following him out into the late-afternoon sunshine. The temperature had dropped a couple of degrees, and it was most pleasant walking up the gravel track outside my house as it snaked between vineyards and olive groves. Oscar repeatedly brought me sticks and pine cones so that I could throw them as far as possible for him to chase, locate and retrieve. Like most Labradors, he has inherited the retriever gene – as well as the gluttony gene.

We had gone only a few hundred metres when my phone started ringing. I pulled it out of my pocket and saw that it was Virgilio, my best friend here in Tuscany.

'*Ciao*, Dan, I've got a suggestion for you. How would you and Anna feel about a week's holiday next month? I'm due some leave, and Lina and I were wondering if you felt like joining us.'

'*Ciao*, Virgilio. A holiday is probably what I need. I'm feeling a bit jaded.'

The idea of a week off certainly had its attraction. Although my two murder mysteries were selling pretty well, it was my day job that paid the bills. I had set up a private investigation agency nearly two years earlier and this had been a remarkably busy year so far. Although it was only May, I had already been involved in all manner of cases, ranging from theft to disappearing persons, marital infidelity to drug addiction, and even murder. The murder investigations had mostly been in collaboration with Virgilio in Florence, which is where I have my office. Although his English is pretty fluent, he often calls me in when a case involves English speakers. He's a *commissario* – roughly equivalent to detective chief inspector – which was the rank I had occupied at the Metropolitan Police in London before taking early retirement and moving here to Tuscany almost three years ago.

I felt sure a week off would do me good and might even help me break out of my writer's block. Apart from anything else, I hoped that Anna would appreciate a week without me going off to 'play detectives', as she put it. I knew that I owed it to her to give both of us a break.

'Where are you thinking of going?'

'Elba. Do you know it?'

'The island where Napoleon was exiled to.'

'That's the one. Have you already been there?'

I had never visited the island of Elba but, like most people, I'd heard of it, and it was definitely on my bucket list of places to visit. The island is just off the west coast of Tuscany, barely ten kilometres from the mainland, and it has become one of Italy's most desirable holiday destinations. From where I lived, just outside Florence, it would probably take only a couple of hours to drive to the little port of Piombino, and there we could catch the ferry to the island. A week there sounded perfect, and I was quick to agree with his suggestion.

'I certainly know of it, but I've never been there. A week lying on the beach sounds like a great idea. It's not very big, is it? Have you got anywhere particular in mind?'

'There's a hotel on the east of the island. I've never been there, but apparently, it's right on the coast with its own private beach and – Oscar will like this – it's dog friendly. Even better, my cousin works there and she says she can do us a good deal.'

'Sounds like a useful cousin.'

'Very useful. To be honest, although I call Rita my cousin, she's actually the daughter of one of my cousins – does that make her my second cousin? – and I haven't seen her for years. The last time I saw her was at her mother's funeral nine or ten years ago – she lived on Elba and the funeral was held there. Rita lost both her parents to cancer in the space of a few months, and we've rather lost touch since then. I knew she was living on the island so I gave her a call, and she's been very helpful.'

'Excellent. You said next month. Any dates in particular?'

'July and August are always very busy, but the first week of June –

before the schools break up – should be a lot less frenetic than high summer.'

I had already come across the phenomenon of the Italian summer holiday. Many businesses close down completely for weeks in summer – particularly in August – and holiday resorts can get seriously overcrowded – without even starting to factor in the millions of visitors from overseas. Early June sounded great. 'I'll have to check with work, but I'm pretty sure I can take a week off, and obviously, I'll need to check with Anna, but hopefully, things will have quietened down for her as well by then.' I thanked him for the invitation and told him I'd get straight back to him once I'd spoken to her.

Of course, this would mean closing the doors of Dan Armstrong Private Investigations for a week, seeing as Virgilio's wife, Lina, was my sole employee, and we would both be away at the same time. Lina acted as my PA, receptionist, telephonist, keeper of the diary, occasional dog walker, and was generally responsible for the office and what happened there. A quick phone call confirmed that she could easily rearrange things for me so as to free us both for the first week of June, so I phoned Anna at home to see how she felt about it. She's a lecturer in medieval and Renaissance history at Florence university and I knew that the academic year would be coming to an end pretty soon. When I floated the idea of Elba past her, she sounded very keen and confident she could get the time off. But then she came up with an idea of her own.

'While on the island, it would be fun if we were to do a windsurfing course. How's that for a suggestion? I'm sure you'd love it.'

I hesitated, telling her I'd think about it, while Oscar and I completed our walk.

The reasons for my hesitation were twofold. First, I was born and bred in London and, although I'd learned to swim in the local public pool, I had little experience of the open sea and none whatsoever of sailing in any of its iterations. Secondly – and secretly this was the one that worried me the most – I would be fifty-eight in a month's time and I wasn't sure that taking up a new and probably energetic hobby at my ripe old age was to be recommended.

I glanced down at Oscar again. He was standing patiently at my feet with an old vine root in his mouth, clearly waiting for me to throw it for him to retrieve. What Virgilio had said about the hotel having its own private beach would suit my big, black Labrador perfectly. I might be a bit hesitant about splashing around in the sea but I knew that Oscar, given the opportunity, would love it.

I reached down, took the gnarly lump of dark-brown wood from Oscar's mouth and flung it as far into my neighbour's olive grove as I could. As he scampered off to collect it, I looked around and found myself smiling appreciatively. My little house in the hills to the southwest of Florence is set in some spectacular scenery. All around me were vineyards with row after row of vines laid out with mathematical precision and olive groves where the dusty leaves of century-old trees provided dappled shelter from the warm, Tuscan sun. Today had been hot for mid-May and even now, at six o'clock in the evening, the shade was welcome. For me and for my dog.

Thought of the time reminded me that Anna was doing a risotto, and I had been warned on pain of death not to be late. Anna and I had been living together for a year now, and things were going really well between us. Following the break-up of my marriage a few years back, and my radical decision to move from London to Tuscany, things had been looking up for me, and Anna was one of the best things to happen to me for a long time.

My thoughts were interrupted when Oscar burst out of the undergrowth in front of me, bearing the root proudly in his teeth. As I took it from him, I caught his eye.

'And you're one of the best things to happen to me as well, Oscar.'

He wagged his tail, but he was clearly far more interested in the vine root.

I patted his head. 'And now, dog, we need to get home for dinner.'

Without hesitation, he immediately turned and started trotting back downhill again. When it comes to food, his linguistic ability is second to none – and that's in Italian as well as English.

By the time we got back home, I had made up my mind. I went over to where Anna was stirring the risotto and kissed her on the back of the neck.

'Elba it is. And if you're serious about the windsurfing, I'm prepared to give it a go.'

She turned towards me and beamed, repeating what she'd said before. 'You'll love it, I'm sure.'

She might be sure, but I wasn't. I intercepted a sceptical look from Oscar that said quite clearly that he wasn't so sure either. Still, I told myself, it would give Anna and me some time together away from our busy working lives, and that had to be a good thing – as long as I didn't drown in the process.

2

SATURDAY 2 JUNE

The drive from Florence that Saturday was uneventful and we took the three o'clock ferry from the port of Piombino to Elba. The island was clearly visible from the mainland as a dark-green, seriously hilly lump sticking up from the deep blue of the pleasantly calm sea. It took barely an hour to get us and a boatload of other vehicles across to Portoferraio, the main town of the island. As we pulled in, Anna the historian pointed out an elegant, cream-coloured villa on the promontory at the entrance to the harbour. This charming, large building, with what looked like an equally lovely garden, had been where Napoleon had been sent in exile. He had subsequently escaped and started up the war again, but, from what I could see, it struck me that settling down here to a peaceful life would have been far more sensible and enjoyable – but dictators do what dictators do.

Portoferraio was a bustling little place built around a horseshoe-shaped bay that formed a perfect natural harbour. Yachts of all sizes, ranging from economy to luxury, including some larger cruise ships, were moored up all the way around the bay, and much of that was lined with three- and four-storey buildings in a delightful mixture of white, cream, ochre and pink colours. Behind these, the ground sloped sharply upwards and the hills behind the town were dotted with red-roofed houses. Close to the ferry port, I was delighted to see a number of fishing boats with people working on and near them. Although tourism had taken over as the main business of the island, at least there appeared to be a healthy fishing fleet still here – and that boded well for some good meals.

It was barely a twenty-minute drive from there to our hotel on the coast not far from the chic resort of Porto Azzurro. Although we were on a main road, in places, it was barely wide enough for two vehicles to pass, and I rapidly discovered that the drivers of the island's buses felt that they had priority over everybody else. Nevertheless, we got to our destination safely just after four-thirty and checked in.

Hotel Augustus was a charming boutique hotel only a stone's throw from the sea. It would normally have been far from cheap, but Virgilio's cousin hadn't been exaggerating when she had told him she could offer us a great deal. The building itself was relatively modern and not of great architectural interest, but its location right on the coast overlooking the sea was delightful. The hotel was on the outside edge of the picturesque village of Santa Sabina sull'Elba, where sun-bleached pink and ochre houses clustered around an ancient, white church that was almost dwarfed by a pair of magnificent umbrella pines that looked even older than the church.

Virgilio's cousin, Rita, was behind the reception desk and she greeted him and the rest of us warmly. She introduced us to the owner, an elderly gentleman called Signor Silvano, who came out of his office, shook our hands, patted Oscar on the head, and then immediately went outside for a smoke. Rita was probably in her mid or late thirties, and she told us that she had been born in the nearby village and she loved the place. By the sound of it, old Signor Silvano had more or less handed over management of the hotel to her, and she was clearly enjoying being almost her own boss.

The first thing we did after getting to our rooms was to change into our swimming things and head for the beach. The grounds of the hotel ran right to the clifftop and included a tiny private cove with a strip of sand little more than the size of a tennis court. Access to it was via a sloping path that zigzagged its way down the steep, rocky hillside between two vertical cliffs that looked as much as ten metres high or even more. The water was crystal clear and I spotted flashes of silver as shoals of little fishes flitted about. It looked as though the seabed shelved steeply until it disappeared into the deep blue of the Mediterranean, or, to be precise, the Tyrrhenian Sea. The water by the shore was an amazing translucent aquamarine colour and we could clearly make out darker patches of weed or rocks on the bottom far below. It was a delightful sight.

We were making our way down the path when a man came running up it. As he approached us, I could hear him panting with the exertion – and on a boiling-hot summer day like this, I wasn't sure this was a sensible thing for him to be doing. As he barged past, it was immediately clear that this was no jogger out for a run. This guy was probably almost sixty like me and he was clearly out of condition. He was wearing a pair of garish, red and orange, Hawaiian-style swimming shorts and his flabby stomach bounced about as he ran. His face was even redder than his shorts and, from the expression on his face, he was either terrified or furious with somebody or something. Whatever it was that had bugged him, I hoped it wasn't going to give him a coronary.

Virgilio turned and surveyed the man's retreating figure as he disappeared up the path, before catching my eye.

'Now, there's an unhappy man if I ever saw one. What he needs is a holiday.' He grinned at me and I nodded in agreement.

'Either a holiday or an ambulance. I'm all in favour of physical exercise, but I have a feeling he might regret this.'

We carried on down to the beach and found that we were to be almost the only people on it. There was just one lone woman over at the far end by a rocky headland. She was sitting on a towel, lighting a cigarette. An unoccupied towel laid out beside her appeared to indicate that this had belonged to the running man. I wondered if they had had a major bust-up. In such an idyllic situation on such a beautiful summer's day, I found myself wondering what might have caused his rapid departure. No sooner had I thought it than I gave myself a mental ticking-off. This was no business of mine, and for the next week, I was not a detective but a holiday-maker here for a bit of R & R with my partner, my close friends and, of course, my dog.

Anna had made it clear that I would do well to remember that I had promised to switch off any investigative instincts I might have from the moment I had arrived here on the island, and I intended to do my best to obey. Besides, as I told myself, maybe a few days away from being a private investigator might help me concentrate more on the conundrum facing my fictional inspector in San Gimignano in my whodunnit.

Oscar, clearly untroubled by any conjecture about the unhappy couple, shot me a brief glance and then made a beeline for the sea, splashing into the water where he was soon doggy-paddling about happily, snuffling and snorting to himself, with just his head and the tip of his tail visible.

I turned to Anna and pointed to him.

'There's definitely something about Labradors and water, isn't there?'

She smiled in response. 'He's not silly, your dog, especially on a day like today. I'm going straight in to join him. You coming?'

Less than a minute later both of us were in the sea, basking in the refreshing – but by no means cold – water. I heard splashing alongside me as Oscar came paddling up to us and tried to climb onto my shoulders. This resulted in both of us disappearing underwater and I was spluttering by the time I came back up again.

'Oscar, for crying out loud, would you leave me alone and go and play somewhere else?'

He didn't look in the least bit repentant, and a thought occurred to me. I took a deep breath, duck-dived down to the steeply sloping seabed and picked up a nicely rounded stone a bit smaller than a tennis ball. Back in the open air, I attracted Oscar's attention and threw it into the shallows for him to chase. He swam off happily and spent the next couple of minutes ferreting about, repeatedly dipping his nose underwater, until he emerged, triumphant, with the stone – or one that looked very much like it – in his mouth. While Anna and I floated idly about, enjoying the peace and quiet, Oscar repeatedly brought the stone for me to throw for him. I had a feeling he was going to sleep well tonight.

A little while later, a noise made me turn my head and I saw a boat appear around the headland. There were two people on board and the boat was heading for the beach. The driver killed the motor as the bow of the inflatable dinghy grounded, and the young woman at the front of the boat jumped over the side and started to pull it up the beach. Her companion joined her and together, they tugged the dinghy clear of the water, after which the man left her and hurried up the path towards the hotel. A plaintive yap revealed that there was a third passenger on board the dinghy. The woman reached in, lifted out a sausage dog and placed it on the sand beside the boat. As she did so, I saw Oscar start swimming over to investigate. Just in case he was to be too playful with this new canine friend a quarter of his size, I followed him in to the shore.

Oscar emerged from the water and shook himself vigorously before padding across to the new arrival and her dog. She was sorting out the things in the boat – among which I could see wetsuits and oxygen cylinders. They had evidently been diving. I had done a diving course some years back while on holiday in Tenerife and had enjoyed it immensely. To be honest, I would really have preferred to be doing that tomorrow rather than a windsurfing course, but it hadn't been my decision. I felt sure that poking around underwater in what I knew to be the protected waters of a marine national park was likely to be fascinating. Still, I told myself, maybe the windsurfing would work out okay...

As I approached the dinghy, I could see that the dachshund was no longer in the full flush of youth and it turned towards Oscar with an expression on its face that I recognised. It was the look to which my mother used to subject me if I had the audacity to disturb her while she was listening to her beloved *Archers* on the radio. I kept a close eye on Oscar, but he behaved like a real gentleman, slowing down and approaching cautiously and respectfully, his tail wagging slowly. The two dogs touched noses and I was relieved to see the little dog's tail also begin to wag. It would appear that peace had broken out.

'What a beautiful Labrador. What's his name?' The woman produced a little smile. She was probably in her early to mid-thirties and she looked fit, with a no-nonsense, short hairstyle. The detective in me noted that she wasn't wearing a wedding ring but, of course, that meant nothing and, besides, hadn't I just taken a vow to stop noticing that sort of thing? She made no attempt to address me in Italian, and her English was very fluent with maybe a hint of a German accent. I smiled back and replied in English.

'This is Oscar. What's your dog's name?'

'Her name is Edith and she's an old lady now.' She shot an affectionate glance down at the dog, who was unsuccessfully trying to stretch high enough to sniff Oscar's butt. 'She's fourteen.'

I indicated the gear in the boat. 'Can I give you a hand?'

She shook her head. 'Thanks, but it'll be fine. We leave the diving gear in the boat. It's a private beach and very secure.' I saw her eyes flick up to the clifftop, but her companion had already disappeared from sight. 'If Martin wants anything, he'll come and get it.'

I left her to what she was doing and headed back to where Anna and the others were busy setting up camp. Virgilio, always well prepared, reached into a cool box and handed me a bottle of cold beer. 'Fancy a drink?'

'Definitely, thanks.' I screwed off the top and took a long, satisfying draught before turning my attention to Oscar, who was waiting patiently at my feet. I pulled out his bowl from my backpack along with a bottle of water, filled it and handed it down to him. Sipping my beer, I sat down beside Anna on a towel looking out to sea while Oscar slurped happily on the other side of me. As we were on the east coast of the island, I could just make out the shape of the mainland of Tuscany through the heat haze across the water. The late-afternoon sun was coming from behind us and Lina and Virgilio had wisely chosen a spot in the shade of the cliff so that we didn't overheat.

'Dan, are you and Anna really going to do a windsurfing course?' Lina sounded sceptical – and I knew how she felt. 'Have you done it before?'

I was just starting to shake my head when I got a considerable surprise. Anna, it appeared, wasn't a novice like me after all, but this was the first I was hearing of it. 'When I lived in England, my ex-husband was keen on windsurfing and I used to do a bit. I haven't touched a board since the divorce years ago, so I've probably forgotten everything.'

I gave her an accusing look. 'And there I was thinking that we would both be beginners together. I'm sure you'll run rings round me.'

She reached over and patted my arm. 'You'll pick it up in no time, I'm sure.'

I decided not to dignify that with a response and just gave Lina a helpless look. 'What can I do? When Anna says jump, I jump. She's a terrible bully, you know.' I softened my words with a smile and a wink towards

Anna and turned the question back on Lina. 'And what are you two going to do while I'm trying not to drown?'

Virgilio answered for both of them. 'As little as possible: swimming, sunbathing, a few gentle walks and a whole lot of eating. The restaurant here has a very good reputation and we can investigate some of the other restaurants in the area as well.'

I gave a resigned sigh. 'That's my kind of holiday...'

Footsteps behind us made me turn my head and I saw two men come down the path to the beach carrying towels. They dumped these on a handy rock and headed straight for the water. As they passed us, I gave them a smile and a nod of the head but received nothing in return. Neither even acknowledged my presence. I was struck by the similarity between them, but I don't mean that they looked alike. Very much the opposite, in fact. One had deep-olive-coloured skin and a shaved head. The other had even paler skin than mine, and his close-cropped hair was a bright carrot colour. But the similarity was in their build and their uncommunicative expressions. Both were tall and muscular, but not with cosmetically sculpted muscles as a result of long hours in the gym. These two were just big, strong men, maybe in their thirties, and as well as looking fit, they looked decidedly dodgy.

'Dodgy' was a term the officers around me at the Met had often used to describe people who looked suspicious. I might have been doing these two a terrible injustice, but my initial impression of them wasn't favourable. What, I wondered, were a couple of hard nuts like this doing here in a luxury boutique hotel? As I'd tried many times to explain to Anna, being a detective isn't something I can just switch on and off. In spite of my vow to take a break from sleuthing, I couldn't help wondering whether these two dodgy-looking guys and the worried man running up the path from the beach might be connected in some way – and, if so, whether this might impact our happy holiday. Anna has often reminded me that crime – and even murder – seems to follow me around wherever I go. Surely not here in this idyllic place.

As they dived into the water and swam strongly out to sea, Virgilio and I exchanged glances and he commented first, his brain no doubt working along the same lines as my own.

'Do you think there's something in the air here? First, that guy comes charging up the path with a face like thunder, and now these two characters show up. I've seen happier-looking corpses.'

I nodded in agreement. 'Mind you, I wouldn't want to pick a fight with either of them, but you're right, they don't seem to have embraced the holiday spirit.' I caught his eye and grinned. 'Maybe the food here at the hotel isn't as good as you think.'

He adopted a horrified expression. 'Don't say that. Please don't let it be that.'

3

SATURDAY EVENING

Dinner that evening cleared the chef of any involvement in stirring up discord. It was excellent. We sat outside on a panoramic terrace with palm trees at either end and a glorious rambling rose on the wall behind us filling the air with its heady scent. From here, we could see the twinkling lights of the coast reaching for miles into the distance. The recent sunset was obscured from view by the rugged hillside behind us and the sky above was a deep claret colour, the tables on the terrace submerged in the shadows by now. The waiter had set a candle on our table to provide light and, as there wasn't a breath of wind, the flame barely moved – apart from when one of us laughed. And we did a lot of laughing. Certainly, it would appear that our table at least hadn't been afflicted by the moodiness affecting some of the other guests.

As this was our first night, Anna and I had insisted on treating Virgilio and Lina to the *menu gastronomico* to thank them for making all the arrangements. As we were on an island, I had been expecting a seafood feast, but along with the fish were some Tuscan staples like pasta and grilled meats. While we were surveying the different dishes on the 'gastronomic' menu, I gradually came to terms with the fact that we were not expected to make a choice between them – we were going to be served *all* of them, drinks included. The waiter brought us glasses of sparkling wine and a bowl of water for Oscar, who, although he had just had his dinner, was positioned between Anna and me, sitting to attention, his head to one side. He appeared to be listening with appreciation as Virgilio read out the list of delights awaiting us and I knew full well that, given the chance, he would have ordered a double helping of everything.

As I sipped my spumante – I'm not really a fan of sparkling wine but it came as part of the *menu gastronomico* package – I looked around at my fellow diners and spotted a few familiar figures. I counted fifteen tables, but only half a dozen were occupied. Rita at Reception had told us that this was their last quiet week before this summer season took off next weekend when school holidays started. From then on, the hotel was fully booked until mid-September.

A few tables from us, I could make out the woman with the dachshund with her companion, and beyond them, the man who had come stomping up the path. He was sitting at a table for two with his female companion, nursing a glass of red wine, while she enjoyed a pre-dinner cigarette. They weren't doing a lot of talking, but at least this meant that his exertions in the hot sun hadn't affected his health. There was no sign of the two hard nuts – as I had notionally labelled them – but at least some of the other diners sounded more cheerful.

In particular, there was a group of four people who were clearly enjoying themselves immensely. Waves of laughter came wafting across from time to time and, along with the merriment, there was the unmistakable sound of British voices. Even in the candlelight, it was clear to see that two of the guests at that table hadn't been using enough suncream, and there was one man in particular whose bald forehead was positively glowing. I hoped for his sake that he wasn't going to have any unpleasant repercussions as a result.

Alongside this group was a table set for three, but with only two people – a man and a woman – presumably sitting and waiting for their companion to put in an appearance. Apart from them, there was just a younger couple towards the far end, no doubt enjoying the romantic setting of the hotel and the warm summer's evening, and beyond them, a table with just one lone diner. It was hard to tell in the candlelight, but I thought he looked East Asian in appearance.

Our antipasti arrived on a trolley laden with individual dishes, and we soon worked out that the waiter was intent on piling a bit of everything onto our plates. Although I enjoy my food – obviously not as much as Oscar, of course – I knew I had to pace myself, so, although I did my best to take a little of everything, I did try to limit the size of the servings. Even so, by the time the waiter moved off again, all four of us were staring at plates groaning with food. The waiter had respectfully murmured the names of the various dishes as he had served them, but I hadn't been able to understand everything he said. As a result, I picked up my fork and embarked on a voyage of discovery.

Silence settled around the table as we all began to sample the delights on offer, the quiet only broken from time to time by mournful murmurs from Oscar, whose nose had no doubt already picked up exactly what was on our plates and even identified the ingredients of the accompanying sauces. I handed him down a couple of breadsticks and he settled on the floor with a sigh. I felt sorry for him being excluded from this feast, but I knew him well enough by now to recognise that I had to harden my heart. Oscar, like most Labradors, would happily eat until he explodes.

Among the amazingly tasty selection of antipasti was the chef's take on bruschetta. In Florence, this tends to be slices of bread topped with chopped tomatoes or chicken liver pâté, but here on the island, the toppings were a wonderful smoked fish mousse, slices of grilled aubergine, and chopped squid in a cheesy sauce. Along with these were stuffed mussels in their shells, grilled anchovies, slices of cured ham and orange-fleshed melon, tiny little octopus in a spicy sauce and a whole lot more.

We drank white wine from mainland Tuscany. The waiter apologised for the lack of truly local wine, telling us that wine production here on the island had shrunk tenfold over the past fifty years as tourism had overtaken fishing, mining and agriculture as the main industry. Although the wine he served us was not from the island, he was able to point across the sea towards the lights of the Tuscan vineyards responsible for producing it, barely twenty kilometres away in the gathering dusk. Whatever its origin, it was a lovely, crisp, dry wine that went perfectly with the antipasti.

By the time we had finished our starters, I was seriously beginning to question whether I would be able to finish everything on the menu. In true

Italian tradition, the antipasti were followed by the pasta course or *primi piatti* – first dishes – as they call them. Once again. the trolley arrived, this time with a selection of different pasta dishes ranging from *fusilli ai frutti di mare* – the pasta almost submerged beneath a rich, creamy sauce containing shellfish and crustaceans – to a local speciality of black risotto. This unusual-looking dish was made using squid ink to turn the white rice black and was dotted with pieces of fish and shellfish, giving it a questionable look, but a wonderful taste of the sea.

After the *primi piatti*, we moved onto the *secondi piatti* and this time, the waiter brought a massive T-bone *Bistecca alla Fiorentina* which he sliced vertically and divided between us, along with a selection of grilled vegetables. This was accompanied by a fine, rich, red Chianti Classico, whose label told me it had in fact been produced less than twenty kilometres from my house.

It was as we were tasting this that things suddenly got weird.

Out of the corner of my eye, I saw one of the people on the table of three stand up and start walking in our direction. He was a big man and, from his unstable gait, it looked as though he'd been drinking heavily. Sensing something in the air, Oscar roused himself from dreams of Florentine steaks, squirrels and swims in the sea, and stood up, his nose pointing inquisitively at the newcomer as he approached our table. The man lurched to a halt behind Virgilio's shoulder and, before any of us could do or say anything, he suddenly reached forward and tipped Virgilio's glass of red wine into his lap. Virgilio looked up in surprise, pushed back his chair and was about to leap to his feet when the man's right hand caught him by the shoulder and pushed him back down.

'You need to be more careful, Sergeant. That was terribly clumsy. You'd better look out or something bad could happen to you… something really bad.' He spoke Italian with a strong Tuscan accent and the menace in his voice was at odds with his summery blue and white shirt and shorts. He was probably about ten years younger than me, with tattoos on both forearms, and it was clear from his muscular build that he kept himself fit. Virgilio is a strong man, but I could see that the pressure of the man on his shoulder was preventing him from making a move.

So I did it for him.

I jumped to my feet and reached across to catch the big man by the arm, doing my best to make him release his grip on Virgilio. 'What the hell do you think you're doing?' I must confess to using an Italian expression that was a whole lot ruder than that.

The man turned towards me and fixed me with a malevolent stare. 'Take your hand off me or I'll snap you in two.' His tone was as aggressive as his alcohol-filled breath, but I'd been up against tougher men than him in my time.

In response, I let my hand slide down his arm to his right hand so that I could grip his fingers and squeeze while pressing my thumb hard down between his thumb and forefinger. This was a useful little trick that I'd learned from a gnarled old London copper called Sergeant Donnelly thirty years ago, and I could see that it hurt the man a lot, but he stubbornly refused to relinquish his hold on Virgilio. He snarled and I could see him pull his other arm back as a precursor to trying to punch me, but I kept the pressure on his hand and used my other hand to grasp the neck of the wine bottle on the table in front of us. To an accompaniment of ferocious growling from my normally pacific dog, I looked the man straight in the eye.

'I wouldn't do that if I were you.' I tried to make my tone as threatening as possible. 'I don't know who you are, I don't know what you've been drinking, smoking or injecting, but you're going to go away now and leave us alone, otherwise things will not turn out well for you. I can do a lot of damage with this bottle. Do I make myself clear?'

There was a brief standoff for a couple of seconds before the man released his grip on Virgilio's shoulder, spat out a stream of invective and turned away. I released his hand and watched as he made his unsteady way back across the terrace once more. As he did so, I had the satisfaction of seeing him massaging his left hand with his right.

I turned back and saw that Virgilio was now on his feet, an expression of deep loathing on his face. I felt a double movement at my side as Oscar pressed his nose against my right leg and Anna reached over to catch hold of my left hand and gently disentangle my fingers from the neck of the wine bottle. Lina was also on her feet, both hands on her husband's arm, a look of deep concern on her face. I was conscious of my heart pounding in my chest as the realisation that I had come close to a potentially very nasty fight registered with me. Along with a feeling of satisfaction that my intervention had successfully defused the situation, there was relief that things hadn't turned any uglier. As Anna never ceased reminding me, the older I got, the more vulnerable I was becoming. I glanced down and was mildly surprised to see the skin of my knuckles stretched white. The atmosphere was electric and the silence was finally broken by Virgilio himself.

'Thanks, Dan. I'm sorry about that.' I saw him give Lina a reassuring look. 'It's all right, it's all over now.'

I gave them both a little smile and sat back down again, feeling the tension start to melt away while the adrenalin still coursed through my body. 'You're welcome. Feel like telling us what that was all about?'

He stood there for a few moments, staring across the terrace before, reluctantly, sitting down again and using his napkin to dry himself off. Interestingly, in the twilight, nobody else appeared to have noticed this little cameo and the holiday mood continued around us – at least among those who had been in the mood in the first place. Virgilio picked up his empty wine glass and returned it to a vertical position before reaching for his water glass and draining it. Finally, he launched into an explanation.

'That animal was Ignazio Graziani, one of the foulest individuals who ever walked on the surface of this planet.' The disgust in his voice was almost palpable. 'Just over twenty years ago, there was a spate of abductions and rapes near Pisa. I was a young sergeant stationed there at the time. It took us three months of hard work, but we finally nailed him. He kidnapped a total of four young women, did unspeakable things to them, before abandoning them in the wilds of the countryside more dead than alive. I was involved in the investigation that led to his arrest, trial, and sentencing to twenty-five years in prison. I was appalled to hear that he'd been released last month – would you believe because he was deemed to be "no longer a risk to the public"? I'd forgotten that he was originally from Elba, and I certainly wasn't counting on running into him ever again.' He relapsed into silence while I picked up the wine bottle and refilled his glass. He looked as though he needed it.

We resumed our meal but I, for one, barely tasted it. Even the panna cotta smothered in caramel sauce and whipped cream, scattered with fresh raspberries and blueberries, failed to hit the spot. By the time our coffees arrived, I was wondering if Graziani had already made the acquaintance of the other guests and if he was responsible for the bad mood of the people on the beach. Might there be some connection between Graziani and the dodgy-looking characters we had seen earlier? Certainly, he had managed to cast a definite shadow over *our* evening.

As I sat there, I realised that I was already filing this confrontation away in my memory banks to be included in one of my whodunnits. That's the wonderful thing about being an author – real life so often throws up fascinating situations every bit as good as fiction. At this point, I had no idea when or where I would draw on this evening's fracas, but I knew I would. Sooner or later.

After dinner, I took Oscar for a walk, accompanied by Virgilio after he had run upstairs to change into a fresh pair of shorts. The grounds of the hotel were surrounded by a solid chain-link fence taller than me, and there was a pedestrian gate off to one side near the clifftop with a key code to restrict access only to guests of the hotel. We opened the gate and followed a footpath that ran southwards through clumps of pine trees, not far from the cliff edge. Apart from a delightful scent of resin, the trees also produced a regular supply of pine cones for me to throw for Oscar to retrieve.

Without the presence of our two partners, Virgilio went into more detail of what Graziani had done to his unfortunate victims and, in spite of our outstanding meal, I could feel a sour taste in my mouth. Virgilio had actually been part of a three-man team who had found one of the distraught victims, barely conscious, badly bruised and beaten, and it was clear that the appearance of this brutally mistreated woman had burned itself forever into his psyche. Ignazio Graziani was a monster, and all four of his victims – although they had survived – undoubtedly still bore psychological as well as physical scars. As we walked along the path, the only sounds the gentle hiss of the tiny wavelets on the beaches below and the background whirring of cicadas in the pines, I felt a million miles away from such depravity – and yet I knew that the perpetrator was sitting having his dinner barely ten minutes away from us. I asked the obvious question.

'What are you going to do about Graziani? That was quite definitely assault by him on you. If he's just come out of jail, I imagine he's on parole. His parole officer isn't going to like that one bit. A few words from you could see him back inside, surely.'

It took a while before Virgilio replied. 'I've been wondering about that. It was dark on the terrace and I don't think anybody else was aware of the scene at the dinner table. If Graziani has a good lawyer, it should be easy enough to point out that the only witnesses were our group and it wouldn't be hard to make a case for us inventing the whole thing – calling it police harassment. After all, there's not a mark on me, but I wouldn't mind betting that his hand is going to be bruised in the morning. You could end up with a charge of assault yourself.'

He had a point, of course, but it didn't seem fair to let the man get away with it. 'Surely if you don't get the police involved, it could be that Graziani's going to spend the next week here and you're going to be seeing each other every day. Sooner or later, that could lead to another confrontation.'

Virgilio stopped and turned towards me. 'Part of me would really like that. Nothing would give me more pleasure than to beat him to a pulp.'

I'd never heard Virgilio sounding so bitter and aggressive before and I knew that this was a dangerous way for a senior police officer to talk. Like it or not, the man had done his time, and any further involvement with him could prove seriously detrimental to Virgilio's position. It occurred to me that there was a pragmatic, if unpalatable, solution, and I chose to suggest it before he did.

'You know what I think? High season hasn't started yet, so there should be lots of spare accommodation on the island. Why don't we cancel our booking here and move somewhere different tomorrow, maybe on the other side of the island? I'm sure Rita and her boss would understand under the circumstances. I wouldn't want you to do anything you might regret.'

There was another long pause before Virgilio replied, resignation in his voice. 'You're right, of course, I have a lot more to lose than he does, but in a way, that would be a victory for him.'

'But it doesn't mean it's got to spoil your holiday.' I turned and looked out to sea, the glow of phosphorescence in the water illuminating the scene and a line of distant, orange lights on the mainland framing it. 'Life's too short, Virgilio. Let it go. Let's look for somewhere else tomorrow and do our best to enjoy the rest of our holiday.' I reminded myself that this was supposed to be a relaxing holiday, and it hadn't started out too well. Secretly, I felt sure that the best thing for all of us would be to turn our backs on this hotel – however lovely – and move on.

Reluctantly, Virgilio told me he would sleep on it and decide in the morning.

4

SUNDAY MORNING

I woke up to another clear, blue sky without a single cloud and I had no doubt it was going to be a hot one. Leaving Anna still asleep, Oscar and I crept out early for our morning walk and followed the clifftop path all the way around to the next bay, where Anna and I were scheduled to start our windsurfing course. I had found it hard to get off to sleep the previous night – no doubt because of the testosterone and adrenalin still swirling around in my system – and Anna had been similarly afflicted. As we lay in the dark, she had confessed to me that she'd been terrified that the confrontation might have spiralled out of control.

'He had such awful eyes, that man. I could imagine him being capable of anything.' I felt her shiver so I hugged her to me while she continued. 'I've never seen you like that before, Dan. It was almost like you became a different person. You frightened him, you know. I could see that in his eyes.'

I nodded. 'If it helps, it frightened me as well. It took me back to similar incidents in my past, and not all of them ended well.' I felt her fingers reach for the scar on my left arm where a knife wielded by a man off his head on acid fifteen years earlier had come within a few inches of slicing open my brachial artery. I had told her about that a year ago when she'd spotted it, although I'd done my best to play down the potential severity of the inci-

dent. I caught hold of her fingers and gave them an encouraging squeeze –
considerably gentler than the squeeze I had given Graziani's – and did my
best to cheer her up. 'But this time, there were three of us against one: me,
Virgilio and, of course, Oscar. He wouldn't have let anything happen
to me.'

'I couldn't bear it if something happened to you, Dan.'

I did my best to comfort her by saying that I was far more frightened at
the prospect of the windsurfing course than I was of an Italian villain, but
it had still been quite a while before I heard her breathing relax into sleep.

It had taken me a good bit longer. Unless Virgilio took the sensible
decision to distance himself from Graziani, I had a feeling that further
confrontation would be unavoidable. One thing I knew for sure was that I
would be only too happy if I never saw Graziani ever again.

It was a delightful morning for a walk in the fresh air – still relatively cool
before the heat of the day. Although it was barely half-past seven, I found that
there was already activity at the Elba Windsurfing Academy – the name
written in English on a sign by the track leading down to the beach. It came as
no surprise at all to see a battered old VW camper van – the vehicle of choice of
the surfing community – come bumping down the track and pull up outside a
wooden structure with the words *Surfers Paradise* on a wooden sign hanging
above the door. I smiled to myself at the lack of an apostrophe. My editor would
definitely not have approved. One thing I had very quickly learned in my new
career as a writer of murder mysteries was that thirty years of writing crime
reports had failed to eliminate a depressing number of grammatical errors.

Oscar and I wandered down to the beach where we received a wave and
a friendly greeting from a blonde woman wearing a T-shirt with the word
Mistral across the front. A rack full of boards with the same logo on them
confirmed my suspicion that she was giving the manufacturer a bit of free
advertising. What was interesting was that she didn't greet me in Italian, or
even English, but in fluent German. Virgilio had told me that the island
was very popular with the Germans as a holiday destination, and many of
them had also bought homes here on Elba. I had done some German at
school many years ago and so I was able to take a stab at an appropriate
response, but she must have very quickly worked out that I wasn't a native

speaker and she switched to pretty good Italian, albeit with a German accent.

'*Ciao*, are you here on holiday?'

I answered in Italian. 'Yes, we're staying at the Augustus, and I've somehow managed to get myself signed up for a windsurfing course here later on today.'

Her smile broadened. 'That's great. I look forward to getting you out on the water.' She bent down to stroke Oscar, who was rubbing up against her suntanned legs – he likes the ladies – and she glanced up at me. 'I'm Ingrid. I'm one of the instructors. Who's this guy?'

'He's Oscar and I'm Dan. I've never windsurfed before, so you'll have to promise to be gentle with me.'

She straightened up and grinned. 'Don't worry, I'm sure we'll have you windsurfing like a pro in a very short time.'

'I think there's more likelihood of Oscar learning than me. There's an old English expression about not trying to teach old dogs new tricks, and I'm an old dog nowadays.'

Her eyes opened a bit wider. 'You're English? Wow, you speak great Italian.' She gave me a wink. 'The English don't normally do foreign languages very well.' She had switched seamlessly to excellent English.

I nodded in agreement. 'I'm afraid that's the problem when you come from a country that speaks the world's chosen language of international communication. We get lazy. As for me, I live here now, so it's obvious that I was going to learn the language. By the way, congratulations on your English. Very impressive.'

She smiled at the compliment. 'What do you do, if you don't mind me asking?'

Seeing as I was on holiday and definitely trying to ensure that this week kept Anna and me as far away from work as possible, I omitted to mention my day job. 'I'm a writer. I live near Florence and I write murder mysteries set here in Tuscany.'

'How exciting. You'll have to tell me how to get hold of them. I love murder mysteries.'

A tall man with long, blond dreadlocks emerged from the bar and gave

Ingrid a little wave. She nodded in his direction before holding out her hand to me. 'Looks like I have to go. *Ciao*, Dan, see you later.'

As Oscar and I walked back along the clifftop path, my thoughts returned reluctantly to Ignazio Graziani. Lovely as it was here, I sincerely hoped that Virgilio would have made the sensible decision to change to a different hotel. It had been patently obvious last night that there was no love lost between the two men, and a stand-up fight between them could have done irreparable damage to Virgilio's career. Better to put as much distance between Virgilio and Graziani as possible. It occurred to me that my new friend at the windsurfing school might have some ideas about suitable hotels, but I knew I'd better wait for Virgilio to make his decision before getting anybody else involved.

Back at the hotel, I found Anna and Lina sitting out on the terrace having breakfast. Lina looked as though she still hadn't fully recovered from last night's scene at the dinner table, and I felt for her. Instinctively, I looked across at the other tables to see if there was any sign of Graziani, but his table was empty, and I had a feeling it would probably be some time before he surfaced, almost certainly with a thumping hangover. There was no sign of Virgilio, and Lina told me he'd slept badly and had got up even earlier than I had, telling her he wanted to go for a walk to try to clear his head.

I sympathised but, as the stay-or-go decision wasn't mine to make, I went into the dining room and helped myself to fruit salad and a couple of croissants from the buffet. I asked for a cappuccino, picked up a glass of orange juice, and returned to the terrace. A minute later, a waitress brought me out my coffee and very kindly went off to get a bowl of water for Oscar. When she returned with it, she was also carrying a biscuit and she gave me an enquiring look.

'Do you think your dog might like one of these?'

I swear Oscar nodded his head before I did. I thanked the waitress and she handed the biscuit down to him. He took it very gently but by the time she had turned away and returned to the dining room, he had already swallowed it. He really doesn't take his time and savour his food.

I took a sip of the scalding coffee before asking Lina the all-important question. 'What do you think Virgilio's going to decide to do? Going off and leaving isn't going to feel very good, but I'm convinced it's the sensible course of action.'

She nodded. 'That's what I was telling him last night. By the way, you two had a long walk last night, didn't you?'

'Did we? I seem to remember I was back in our room shortly after ten.'

Lina looked puzzled. 'That's strange. Virgilio didn't come back until past eleven. He must have carried on walking around, trying to get his head straight.'

At that moment, I spotted the man himself. By this time, Oscar had licked up every single crumb – and a few imaginary ones – from the floor at my feet and he jumped up to greet Virgilio. The rest of us looked up with the same unspoken question on our lips, but Virgilio saved us the trouble of asking.

'I finally made up my mind that life's too short, just like Dan told me, and the sensible thing to do is to put as much distance as possible between me and Graziani. I thought I would check first of all to see how long he's planning on staying and I've been to speak to Rita at Reception.' A hint of a smile appeared on his face. 'The very good news is that he isn't staying here at all. He only came here for dinner last night.'

I felt a surge of relief and satisfaction that was obviously shared by Lina. She caught hold of her husband's hand and gave him a beaming smile. 'That's excellent news; we can all relax. Why don't we go with Dan and Anna to watch them windsurfing this morning? We all need a change of scene, don't we?'

I thought it a good idea to get Virgilio away from the hotel, but I must confess that the thought of having an audience while I did my best to balance on a piece of plastic on the ocean wave wasn't very appealing. Still, I told myself, it was a major relief that Virgilio wasn't going to be meeting his nemesis again.

As it turned out, however, we were to see Ignazio Graziani much sooner than we'd thought.

5

SUNDAY MORNING

We were just finishing our breakfast when there was the sound of running feet and I saw the owner of the dachshund come charging up the steps from the garden onto the terrace. She was red in the face and wild-eyed, and I instinctively jumped to my feet to ask her if all was well. She shook her head, took a few deep breaths and broke the news to us.

'I've just been down on the beach and there's a dead body lying on the rocks. It's a man and he must have fallen down the cliff.'

Virgilio was also on his feet by this time. 'You're sure the man's dead? I'm a police officer, by the way.'

She nodded decisively. 'There's no doubt about it. Apart from anything else, his face is underwater so he must be dead.'

'Whereabouts is the body?'

'At the far right side of the beach... that's the south side. Martin and I were getting our things ready for a dive when I saw something flapping in the breeze. I went over to take a look and that's when I saw him. It was horrible.' Her face, which had been red before, visibly drained of colour and Virgilio and I hastily grabbed her arms and guided her onto a seat. Both of us were familiar with the symptoms of shock, and it was clear she had had an awful experience. Oscar, too, picked up on her distress and came over to sit down beside her, a concerned look on his face as he placed one big, hairy paw on her knee in a show of canine support. I sat down alongside her and spoke to her as softly and gently as I could.

'Is your friend Martin still down there?' She nodded her head, and I carried on. 'And what's your name? I'm Dan.'

'Heidi... Heidi Engadin.'

I grabbed a handful of paper napkins from the dispenser on the table and she took them gratefully with a shaking hand as tears started to run down her cheeks. I glanced up at Virgilio, who was reaching for his phone. 'While you call the local police, I'll go and tell the management, okay?' He nodded so I turned to Anna. 'Maybe you might like to keep an eye on Heidi...?'

I left Heidi in Lina and Anna's care and went into the dining room and down the corridor to the main entrance. Rita gave me a welcoming smile. 'Good morning, all well?'

'I'm afraid not.'

I went on to tell her what Heidi had told us and she looked understandably appalled. I told her that Virgilio was in the process of calling the local police and she immediately went off to inform Signor Silvano, the owner. I returned to the terrace and when I got there, Virgilio caught my eye and beckoned to me to follow him. I made my way past the table where Heidi was still sitting with Lina and Anna, and I threw Anna an apologetic glance. She knew and I knew exactly why I was apologising, and I told myself that I would just take a quick look and then leave it to the local police. It didn't matter whether the man had slipped, jumped or been pushed; this death was nothing to do with me, and I was only going along to keep Virgilio company. I repeated this to myself as a mantra all the way down the path to the beach.

This death is nothing to do with me. This death is nothing to do with me. This death...

When we got down to the beach, we received a frantic wave from Heidi's partner, Martin, and we hurried over to where he was standing alongside his inflatable dinghy, looking as shell-shocked as Heidi had been. Even Edith the dachshund was looking subdued. While Oscar wandered over to renew his acquaintance with his canine friend, Virgilio pulled out his warrant card and spoke to the man in English.

'Martin? My name is Virgilio Pisano and I'm a *commissario* in the Florence police force. I've notified the police in Portoferraio and they're sending a squad car straight away. Have you seen the body?'

Martin nodded grimly. 'Yes, it's... he's over there.' He pointed towards a rocky outcrop with little waves splashing against it. 'Not a pretty sight.' Like Heidi, he was fluent in English and probably in his thirties as well.

Virgilio and I left the two dogs with Martin and walked over to the rocks. The light-grey stone had been smoothed by the sea over millennia, and in other circumstances, the scene would have been beautiful, but not this morning. A glance up the cliff face above us told me that the victim had probably suffered a fall of fifteen metres or so – roughly the height of a four- or five-storey building. It was immediately clear that the impact against these rocks had been catastrophic. At least, I told myself, it would have been a very quick death.

The body was lying face down, the broken limbs splayed out on the rocks like a discarded rag doll, with much of the man's head and both arms being washed by little wavelets as Heidi had said. The head and body were badly battered and bruised, and my suspicious mind immediately made me question whether this had been caused during the fall or by an aggressor on the clifftop.

I knew better than to touch a body, but I didn't need to lift the face out of the water to recognise the victim. The tattoos and the summery blue and white shirt and shorts – albeit now badly ripped and stained – were unmistakable. I turned towards Virgilio and saw that he, too, had recognised the victim. He was rooted to the spot, his eyes staring fixedly at the remains of the big man. Slowly, reluctantly, he finally managed to drag his eyes away and he looked across at me with just one word.

'Graziani.'

I nodded. 'Well, that solves our little problem, doesn't it?' I'm not normally so flippant in the face of death but, from what I'd seen the previous evening and from what Virgilio had told me about the man's atrocities, I felt sure that Graziani's death was no loss to humanity.

Virgilio made no reply, his eyes returning to the body on the rocks. I could only imagine the feelings going through his head at the thought that justice for the poor victims had finally been done. I reached over and tapped him on the arm, attracting his attention once more as I pointed back towards Martin and his dinghy.

'I think we need to let Martin go back to the hotel to be with his girlfriend, don't you? Why don't you go with him? I can stay here and make sure nobody goes near the body.'

He shook his head and emerged from his catatonic state. 'It's good of you to offer, Dan, but this is the job I get paid for. Why don't you walk back up with him and I'll wait here until the emergency services arrive? Go on, you accompany Martin back to the hotel, and I'll come up and join you as soon as the police get here and take over.'

I nodded in the direction of the body. 'Are you sure you don't want me to stay with you?'

'I'll be fine.' He glanced up and caught my eye for a moment, and I couldn't miss the strange glint in his. 'It's funny, really. Last night, I would happily have pushed him off the cliff myself, but seeing him here like this doesn't give me a nice, warm feeling of satisfaction. I just feel nothing, nothing at all.'

I've seen a lot of death in my time and I knew exactly how he felt. There's something about the finality of finding a dead body. It somehow wipes the slate clean – but some slates don't deserve to be wiped.

I made no comment but just patted him on the shoulder and then went back to Martin. Together with the two dogs, we walked up the path to the hotel without exchanging a single word. It was only when we reached the top and were approaching the terrace that Martin stopped and looked across at me, a bewildered expression on his face.

'Do you think it was an accident or did he jump?'

There was, of course, another alternative – had he been pushed? From what Virgilio had told me, I could well imagine that a man with Graziani's background could have made a lot of bitter enemies, people with long memories. If I were the investigating officer, I would be checking back through his history along with the backgrounds of the other guests at the hotel, just in case there was anybody with a grudge here, maybe related to one of the man's victims all those years ago. Virgilio's experience of the victim would no doubt be of interest to the police, and I hoped he wouldn't get drawn into the investigation, interrupting his holiday. Maybe I could help...

No sooner had I thought this, however, than I told myself very firmly that I was not the investigating officer, I was not going to become the investigating officer and, indeed, I had no interest in whatever the investigating officer would discover. I was on holiday and that was that.

Anna would have been proud of me – but she would also have questioned to what extent I really meant it. She knows me too well.

In response to Martin's question, I shook my head helplessly, made a few consoling noises and left it at that while I continued my internal monologue.

This death is nothing to do with me. This death is nothing to do with me...

When we got back to our table, Heidi pulled herself to her feet and murmured thanks to Anna and Lina before going off with Martin and the little dog, presumably to their room. I caught the eye of the waitress and ordered an espresso. I raised an eyebrow towards Anna and Lina, but they shook their heads and the waitress went off.

Anna reached across and took my hand. 'Was it awful?'

To be honest, I'd seen far worse, but all I did was shrug my shoulders before breaking the important news to them. 'It wasn't so bad, but it came as a shock all the same. The victim is none other than Ignazio Graziani.' I saw them both look up in surprise, and there was a gasp from Lina as I carried on. 'His body's lying on a rocky outcrop by the beach after a fall from the top of the cliff. He's stone dead.'

'When do you think it happened?'

'I'm no pathologist, but I would imagine quite a few hours ago, some time last night.' I decided not to go into the intricacies of the onset and duration of rigor mortis, especially at the breakfast table. 'He was very drunk when we saw him, so I imagine it might have been an accident. Maybe he decided to go for an after-dinner walk and took a wrong turning.'

Anna knew me well enough by now to recognise the note of doubt in my voice and she made a logical suggestion. 'Or maybe he decided to take his own life. The weight of what he did twenty years ago must surely have been playing on his conscience.'

Lina leant across the table towards us and voiced the other hypothesis. 'Or maybe somebody deliberately pushed him over the edge of the cliff. God knows, it sounds as though he deserved it.'

Determined to respect my resolution to avoid 'playing detectives', I deliberately played this scenario down. 'Who knows? The important thing is that he's gone, and this means we can get on with our holiday.'

I felt Anna's eyes on me and I felt sure I could sense scepticism emanating from her but I avoided looking at her and glanced down at Oscar by my side instead. That didn't help much. If the expression on his face was anything to go by, he wasn't buying my declared lack of interest any more than Anna was. Fortunately, at that moment, we heard the unmistakable wail of sirens as what sounded like at least a couple of vehicles pulled up in the parking area on the other side of the hotel. The waitress brought me my coffee and as I sipped it, I could imagine the scene down on the beach. What, I wondered, would the police and, in particular, the pathologist make of this violent death? Self-inflicted, accidental, or might it really have been murder? I took a deep breath and tried to refocus my mind on a noisy group of seagulls flying overhead rather than the body on the beach.

This death is nothing to do with me, this death is nothing to do with me.

I looked back down at Oscar. That same sceptical expression was still on his face.

I avoided looking at Anna.

6

SUNDAY

The first session of our windsurfing course went really well – for Anna.

As for me, it ranked up there – or should that be down there? – alongside the way I felt the morning after the only time I was ever stupid enough to drink eight pints of beer, the agony of a shoulder dislocated in a rugby match and the first time I came across a decaying corpse.

I should have known that it was going to be grim when Ingrid insisted I put on a wetsuit. Considering that the temperature was already in the high twenties, I protested, but she was right. In the course of the first two-and-a-half-hour session, I lost count of the number of times I fell into the water and had to heave myself back onto the board again. Sunlight or no sunlight, the constantly evaporating water on my skin would have chilled me to the core, and I would soon have got very cold. By the end of the morning, my eyes were burning, I had seawater up my nose, in my ears, and quite possibly swirling around in my brain as well. It's amazing how a solid-looking lump of plastic about eight feet long and two or three feet wide can suddenly become as wobbly as a trapeze. To make matters worse, every time I climbed back onto the board, all I got from Ingrid, who was sitting comfortably in her rubber dinghy looking on, was the instruction to 'relax'.

Some hopes.

Mercifully, we had a break at lunchtime, and I very nearly fell asleep over my non-alcoholic beer and focaccia sandwich. Ingrid, my torturer, had advised me not to drink alcohol in case it made me '*too* relaxed'. I did as I was told, but I felt sure there was no chance of that happening any time soon.

In the beginners' group alongside me were a couple of French university students and the lone diner from our hotel, who I now knew to be called Tatsuo, from Japan, who managed to get the hang of windsurfing quicker than I did. The fact that the combined age of my three companions probably wasn't that much older than me did little to boost my confidence, and if it hadn't been for Anna's insistence and my innate stubbornness, I would probably have headed back to the hotel for a stiff drink and a siesta.

As for Anna, it was clear that her previous experience rapidly came back to her and she was promoted to the advanced class. I occasionally saw her zooming past me with a smile on her face and the wind in her sail, while I either fell into or climbed out of the sea. Our respective performances were keenly observed by Virgilio and Lina at the bar, with Oscar occasionally opening an eyelid from his comfortable position snoozing in the shade. At lunchtime, Virgilio was tactful enough not to talk about windsurfing and, while Anna excitedly recounted her adventures to Lina, he told me quietly what had happened on the beach when the police had arrived.

'The officer in charge is an Inspector Bellini. He's about my age and he's been around a long time. He sounds as if he knows what he's doing and he's already made it clear that this is his case, not mine. I don't blame him. The last thing he needs is an officer from another force trying to horn in on his investigation. I got the feeling he's already convinced himself that it was either an accident or suicide.'

'And he may well be right. What about the pathologist? Did he or she have any observations to make?'

'She's taken the body off to the morgue for an autopsy but, unlike the inspector, her first impression was that foul play may have been involved because of the positioning of the wounds on the body.'

I stretched my aching shoulder muscles and took another big slug of the imitation beer. 'What about you, Virgilio? Have you come to terms with it now? Graziani's gone and that's the end of it. There's no way he can be made to pay any more for what he did, but the simple fact is that Tuscany is a whole lot safer now that he's dead.'

Virgilio nodded. 'Yes, you're right. I'm afraid that seeing him here last night really shook me, and it brought back a load of memories that I'd believed dead and buried.' He picked up his glass and clinked it against mine with a show of enthusiasm – real or fake. 'The holiday starts now, right?'

I glanced apprehensively at my board and rig lying on the sand a few metres away from me and, in spite of the heat, I shivered. 'From my point of view, I think the holiday is going to start at four-thirty when my next lesson ends, assuming I don't drown in the meantime.'

I didn't drown that afternoon and, to my considerable surprise, I finally discovered the trick of staying upright on the board. Ingrid had been dead right. It was fundamentally a matter of trying to relax. Instead of tensing and fighting every slight movement of the board on the water, I gradually learned to go with the flow and let the gentle breeze in the sail move me along.

By the time four-thirty came around, I had been able to sail – albeit awkwardly – from one end of the beach to the other, although any attempt to turn around inevitably ended in disaster. I'm sure I gave considerable amusement to the holidaymakers stretched out on their sunbeds under their parasols. Like most Italian beaches, this one had been carved up into *bagni*, where beachgoers paid a handsome sum for sunbeds, changing rooms and a bar. Still, by the time my day of purgatory finally ended, I had to admit that I might just possibly be beginning to enjoy this windsurfing business – assuming that my arm and shoulder muscles would be up to the task when I woke next day.

Anna and I walked back to the hotel along the clifftop with Oscar running on ahead. Such had been my apprehension before my wind-surfing session, I had committed the deadly sin – in his eyes – of forgetting to bring his lunch with me. Fortunately, the staff at the beach bar had ensured that he didn't fade away by giving him leftover sandwiches, biscuits and at least one packet of potato crisps. I shuddered to think what might be happening to his digestive system by now. One thing was for sure: we would be sleeping with the window open tonight.

Back at the hotel, after giving him his food, I stood under a cool shower for several minutes and gradually did what Ingrid had been telling me to do all day – I relaxed. In fact, I managed to relax so successfully that when I came out of the shower and lay down on the bed for a quick rest, I fell asleep and didn't wake until almost six.

'Feel better?'

I rolled over at the sound of Anna's voice. She was sitting on the bed alongside me, propped up against the headboard with a weighty historical tome in her hands. I gave her a smile. 'Remarkably, yes.' I stretched tentatively. My shoulders ached a bit, but far less than I had feared. 'What about you? Looking forward to tomorrow's session?'

'Definitely, but what about you?'

'If you'd asked me at lunchtime, I'd have run a mile but, all things considered, yes, I think I am looking forward to doing it again tomorrow.' There was a movement from the floor beside me and Oscar's nose appeared by my elbow. 'Our four-legged friend probably needs a walk. You feel like coming?'

She shook her head. 'You go. I'm very comfortable here and, besides, I'm prepping a whole new course for next autumn, so I really need to do a bit of reading while I'm here.'

Oscar and I went out, and I couldn't resist taking a walk down to the beach to see if anything was going on down there. Everything appeared to have returned to normal. The body had been removed, there was no incident tape around the headland where the body had been discovered, and no sign of any members of the police force. Evidently, the investigating officer's hunch that it had been an accident or suicide had been vindicated.

While Oscar splashed around in the shallows, I stood there for a minute or two, wondering what had happened here last night. My brief encounter with Graziani tended to make me think that the most likely explanation for the fall was an accident – caused by an excess of alcohol in his bloodstream – but I couldn't shift the idea that somebody might have assaulted him. His body had been a real mess after the fall, but presumably, the pathologist had been able to work out the true circumstances. I tended to dismiss the idea of suicide as he hadn't struck me as a man bearing such a terrible burden of guilt that he'd decided to end it all. Maybe too much wine, a dark night and a high cliff had been all it had taken.

Inevitably, my mind returned to my current book. Over the last few weeks, I had written and rewritten about ten thousand words without coming up with anything that satisfied me or that would have satisfied a reader. I had even reached the point of considering changing the whole thing and removing the dead body in San Gimignano completely. Now here I was, faced with a situation that didn't differ too greatly from the scene in the book and I wondered if there might be any lessons to be learned from reality that I could incorporate into my fiction.

My literary musings were interrupted when, to my considerable surprise, I heard police sirens arriving at the hotel, and I hurried back up the path to see what was going on. Two squad cars were now parked outside the main entrance and as I approached the terrace with Oscar, a uniformed officer held up her hand and asked for my ID. I wasn't carrying my wallet, but I gave her my name and room number and she checked me off on a clipboard.

'I'm afraid we're going to need fingerprints from everybody here.' She was a young constable and she was being very polite. She pointed to a table a bit further along the terrace. 'If you would like to go and see my colleagues over there, they'll deal with you. It'll only take a minute or so.'

I told her I was happy to oblige and asked the question that was now uppermost in my mind. 'Does this mean that you're now treating the death as suspicious?'

For a second, it looked as though she was going to answer, but then her training kicked in and she just pointed to the table along the terrace once again. 'You can ask my colleagues over there.'

I left her and walked across to where two people were sitting behind a table. One was a uniformed officer with sergeant's stripes on his epaulettes. Alongside him was a dark-haired man, maybe just a bit younger than me, say in his early fifties, wearing a plain, white shirt. He had a suntanned face, an aquiline nose and an air of authority. I assumed this was the investigating officer Virgilio had mentioned: Inspector Bellini. He had a copy of the guest list in front of him and when I gave him my name, he ticked it off and indicated the sergeant.

'I don't know if you ever had your fingerprints taken before, Signor Armstrong, but it's very quick. Sergeant Gallo will see to it.'

I nodded in agreement and took two steps sideways until I was standing in front of the sergeant. He produced an ink pad and card and while he was pressing my fingers onto it, I looked back at the inspector. 'Has the pathologist come up with anything? Presumably, this means you're treating the death as suspicious now?'

I saw him take a closer look at me. 'Can I ask you what your interest is in this matter?'

It was a fair question so I gave him an honest answer. 'Professional curiosity. I used to be in the Metropolitan Police murder squad in London.'

Comprehension dawned on his face. 'You must be the friend of Commissario Pisano. He told me he was here with a fellow officer.' He was sounding polite, but I could see from his expression that he viewed me as a potential pain in the backside, so I did my best to reassure him.

'A *former* fellow officer – I retired three years ago. I now live near Florence and I'm here for a few days' holiday.' I decided not to mention that I was now a private investigator. When I had been at the Met, I had always viewed PIs as potentially bad news – often interfering, and not too worried about how they got results. That wasn't the way I operated, but Bellini had no way of knowing.

'I see.' He hesitated before grudgingly answering my original question. 'The pathologist has been unable to rule out foul play.' From his tone, he didn't share that opinion.

'You think he was murdered?'

Again, he hesitated before finally deciding to answer. 'Personally, no. The cause of death was definitely severe trauma to the head, but the pathologist is bothered that there are wounds to both the front and the back of the skull. As far as I can see, these could have been caused as the victim fell or by the impact when he landed on the rocks, but she thinks it just possible he might have received a blow to the back of the head, after which, the killer pushed the victim over the edge. It's my duty to double-check.'

I got the feeling that he was only going through the motions – maybe on the orders of a superior officer. 'So does the fact that you're taking fingerprints mean that you have a possible murder weapon?'

'No, but we're going to carry out a full search of the clifftop area and I'll have a team of divers here in the morning, checking in case a weapon was thrown out to sea – not that I think there's much hope of finding anything. The pathologist thinks it was a rock.'

The seabed shelved steeply and I also doubted whether the divers would spot anything, so he was probably right to sound sceptical, not least if the murder weapon had been a rock. 'If you find proof of murder, is it your opinion that the killer is somebody at the hotel?'

He nodded. 'If it was murder – and it's a big if – it looks that way. The hotel grounds are protected by a high fence, so it would have been difficult for anybody to get in from outside. There are CCTV cameras inside and outside the hotel and my people are studying the footage closely.'

I glanced down at Oscar, who was sitting to attention alongside me, possibly waiting to have his paw prints taken. 'You'll see me and Oscar – that's my dog – on the CCTV footage. We went for a half-hour walk with Commissario Pisano around half-past nine. Did the pathologist give a time of death?'

'Between ten and midnight.' He looked away and I followed the direction of his eyes to see Tatsuo, my windsurfing companion, approaching. 'Anyway, Signor Armstrong, I'm afraid this means that all of you here are under suspicion until we can rule out foul play, and I'm asking everybody to make sure they stay in the hotel or close by.' He glanced down at Oscar and produced a hint of a smile 'I think we can take it that your dog is in the clear.'

'My partner – that's Anna Galardo – and I are supposed to be doing a windsurfing course at the academy in the next bay tomorrow and subsequent days, between ten-thirty and four-thirty. Is that going to be all right?'

He nodded and made a note on his pad. 'That'll be fine. Thank you for informing me.'

'I'll go and tell Anna to come down to get her prints taken.'

I headed back across the terrace, shooting Tatsuo a little smile of my own as I passed him. It occurred to me that having their fingerprints taken wasn't likely to go down well with some of the less cheerful guests. I wondered what the mood would be like at dinner tonight and I had a feeling the chef was going to have his work cut out to keep everybody happy.

7

SUNDAY EVENING

We had arranged with Lina and Virgilio that we would meet up on the terrace for dinner at eight, but there was a knock on our door at seven-thirty as I was watching Oscar as he finished hoovering up his dinner. I opened the door to see Virgilio standing there, looking serious.

'*Ciao*, Dan. Can you spare me five minutes?'

I glanced over my shoulder and saw that Anna had heard. Oscar had just swallowed the last of his food and was following it with a good slurp of water. Interpreting the invitation as applying to both of us, he headed for the door, tail wagging, to greet his friend. Anna waved me away, and Oscar and I went out into the corridor. I followed Virgilio down to the bar where he ordered two beers, and we took them out into a little piece of garden containing a remarkable collection of prickly pears and other cacti. There was a bench there facing out over the gardens and we sat down side by side. While Oscar wandered around on a tour of inspection, Virgilio absently clinked his bottle against mine and looked up.

'I imagine you've had your prints taken by now?' I nodded and he continued. 'I need to tell you something before...' I had to wait some time before he continued, and what he said came as a considerable surprise '... before Bellini arrests me.'

'Arrests *you*?' Oscar must have heard the disbelief in my voice as he came trotting back to see what was wrong. I tousled his ears as I carried on. 'What on earth for?'

'The murder of Ignazio Graziani.'

I've been faced with all kinds of unusual situations in my life, and not very much surprises me these days, but hearing my best friend – himself a senior police officer – telling me he was going to be arrested for murder certainly came as a considerable shock. Doing my best to keep my voice even, I asked the million-dollar question.

'*Did* you kill Graziani?'

He shook his head. 'Of course I didn't, but the fact is that I haven't been straight with you, or indeed the inspector.' He took a long draught of beer before continuing. 'The thing is, Dan, I saw Graziani again last night after you went to bed.'

'There's a big difference between seeing the guy and killing him. What happened?'

'I needed to clear my head so, after we split up, instead of going back to the room, I went outside again and made my way down to the beach. I sat on a rock for ages, trying to make up my mind whether to stay here or move to another hotel before finally deciding to sleep on it. I came back up the path and when I reached the top, I almost bumped into Graziani. He was leaning against a tree. By this time, my eyes had got used to the dark, and I recognised him immediately. He also recognised me and, without a word, he lurched forward and took a swing at me. He was so drunk that he missed by a mile and almost fell over. I know I should have just left it at that but all the emotion, all the memories – some truly terrible memories that still haunt me – came flooding back and I hit him.' He held out his right hand and I saw his bruised knuckles. 'I only hit him once, on the left cheek, but it was enough to send him flying.'

I could hardly believe my ears. 'And he went over the cliff?'

'God, no. We weren't anywhere near the cliff edge. I just sent him sprawling into the trees and I left him there. From my point of view, it was cathartic, and I could feel myself smiling all the way back to the hotel. All my pent-up disgust and loathing came out in that one blow, and I felt as if a huge weight had been lifted from my shoulders.' He shook his head ruefully. 'I should have told the inspector this but, for some reason –

professional embarrassment, probably – I didn't. The trouble is that I'm sure the CCTV will show him going out and then me going out again. Forensics may even be able to get some of my DNA off his body. It won't take Bellini long to check back and find that I was one of the investigation team when Graziani was carrying out his atrocities. For all I know, somebody maybe saw the little scene with the red wine last night as well. Either way, the finger of suspicion will understandably point at me, and I'm sure he'll arrest me.' He looked up and caught my eye for a moment, his expression one of resignation. 'If the roles were reversed, that's what I'd do – or at least sit him down and lean on him. It's what you'd do as well, isn't it?'

The short answer to that one was probably yes, but I didn't say it. Instead, I was determined to stay positive. 'First, there's a big difference between the CCTV showing you going out and coming back again, and you being seen murdering somebody. Second, I seriously doubt whether they'll be able to pick up any of your DNA on the body. If you hit him in the face, don't forget that much of the man's head and arms spent all night immersed in seawater. Thirdly, there's the question of timing. What time was it when you met Graziani?'

'About eleven. It was ten past when I got back to my room.'

'When I spoke to the inspector earlier on, he told me that the pathologist had come up with a window of between ten and midnight, so that means that there was almost another full hour for the killer to act. So, if there's CCTV footage showing you coming back at just after eleven, in all probability, there will also be footage of the killer, assuming he or she came from the hotel.'

He didn't respond and we both sat there in the evening sunlight trying to think of the best course of action. In fact, it didn't take that long. There was one thing that Virgilio had to do as soon as possible. As he wasn't forthcoming, I decided to spell it out to him.

'You need to see the inspector right now and tell him what you've just told me. Tell him about last night's scene with the red wine and tell him about your part in the Graziani investigation. You are a respectable – and respected – senior police officer and you have nothing to hide.' I tapped him on the arm to attract his attention. 'I mean it, Virgilio; there's no proof you were involved in his death, but the longer you leave it without telling the inspector your full story, the more suspicious it's going to look.'

He nodded gloomily. 'You're right, Dan. I've just been putting it off. It's time to talk to him. I wonder if he and his people are still here.' He swallowed the last of his beer and stood up. 'I'll go and see if they're still on the terrace taking fingerprints.'

I stood up as well and set off around the side of the building with him. We had barely reached the steps to the terrace when Inspector Bellini and the uniformed sergeant appeared in front of us. The sergeant had the decency to look somewhat embarrassed, but there was a gleam of satisfaction in the inspector's eyes as he addressed Virgilio.

'Commissario Pisano, I'm going to have to ask you to come with me to the police station. I have some questions for you about the murder of Ignazio Graziani.'

Virgilio nodded solemnly and glanced across at me. 'Seems like I left it too late after all, Dan.'

The least I could do was to support my friend, so I addressed the inspector directly. 'Commissario Pisano has just been telling me what happened last night, Inspector, and he was on his way to tell you. It may help your investigation, but there's no question of him being involved in murder.'

Bellini gave no response. With Virgilio sandwiched between him and the sergeant, they set off towards the car park, and I called after them. 'I'll tell Lina, Virgilio. Don't worry, it'll all get sorted out.'

Or so I hoped.

Lina and Anna were both sitting at our table and Oscar trotted ahead of me to greet them. Both looked up and smiled, but the smiles didn't last long, even though I tried to put as positive a spin on it as I could.

'Virgilio has gone off to Portoferraio with the inspector. It turns out that he saw Graziani again last night at around eleven and the police want to speak to him about what happened.'

An apprehensive look appeared on Lina's face. 'He's been arrested?'

'No, not at all.' I was trying desperately to sound encouraging. 'He's just helping them with their inquiries.' I groaned internally at my choice of words. How many times in my life had I used this exact same cliché? Technically, I was right, he hadn't been arrested... at least not yet.

One look at Lina's face told me that this didn't come as a total surprise to her. I gave her a few moments to collect herself before asking a gentle question. 'Did he say something to you, Lina?'

She had to clear her throat before answering. 'Not really, but I could tell there was something not quite right with him ever since that awful man came across and spilt wine on him. He's only mentioned him a couple of times since then, but there was real anger in his eyes when he did. What happened to those poor women really got under Virgilio's skin. He didn't tell me that he met the man again last night. What happened between them? He didn't do anything stupid, did he?'

I related what Virgilio had told me, emphasising that there was no proof against him, and ending on a note of optimism. 'I imagine he'll be back here in a couple of hours.' The waiter from last night approached us and I caught Lina's eye. 'I think it would be sensible for us to eat, don't you?' An idea struck me. 'We can ask them to give you a doggy bag for Virgilio, so he has something to eat later on.' As I used the words 'doggy bag,' I sensed interest from my four-legged companion. Like I say, he doesn't miss much when it comes to food.

It was another excellent meal but none of us – apart from Oscar, of course – felt like eating very much. Instead of the gastronomic menu, all three of us opted for just some bruschetta as a starter followed by *cacciucco* – a local speciality fish stew. With big lumps of fish floating in a creamy sauce laced with herbs, this was excellent. Accompanied by fresh bread and cold white wine, and followed by home-made ice cream, it would have been a great meal if we'd been in the mood. But, understandably, we weren't.

Anna was clearly applying her considerable brain to the case and she soon asked the most important question of all. 'We know that Virgilio didn't kill him, so who did – if indeed it wasn't just an accident?'

My mind had been running on similar lines ever since Virgilio had been marched off. 'Inspector Bellini gave me the impression that he thought it was an accident and he's probably just following procedure. If it turns out it was murder, then it's logical to assume that it was somebody here at the hotel, either a member of staff, a guest or one of the diners here last night from outside. Bellini told me the hotel has CCTV capable of picking up anybody trying to get onto the grounds, but I'm not so sure. In my experience, CCTV often has blind spots. In fact, the first thing I'm going to do once I've had my coffee is to go and see if I can plot the field of vision of each of the cameras. I'll start by asking Rita if I can have a look at the images on the screen.'

Anna nodded approvingly. 'Assuming for a moment that it was murder, and the killer is somebody here, who do you think it might be?'

I shrugged my shoulders and, while the waiter brought us our coffees, I looked around the terrace. Tonight, seven tables were occupied, Among them was the table where the victim had been sitting the previous evening, now set for two. The man and woman at that table were hard to make out in the shadows but they were unmistakably the same two from last night. I studied them carefully and, at least from a distance, they didn't appear to have been too badly affected by the death of their former dinner companion. I would dearly have liked to see a guest list and I wanted to see if I could persuade Rita to let me have access to this as soon as I finished my meal. Of course, now that I was no longer an official member of a police force, she was under no obligation to reveal these details to me and, indeed, would be well within her rights to refuse, but this was her cousin – albeit a distant cousin – we were talking about.

The four Brits were at the same table as the previous night but were noticeably less ebullient. The idea that they might be in close proximity to a brutal murderer was no doubt responsible for this. Ingrid and Martin with their dachshund were at a nearby table and, further over, Tatsuo was eating alone as before. Near him was the young couple, still apparently engrossed in each other to the exclusion of all else, but no doubt even they were shaken by recent events. That left the man with the flowery shorts who had come charging up the path towards us. Tonight, he was sitting quietly with his wife or partner, and just past their table, I spotted the two men I had mentally nicknamed the hard nuts. Last night, they hadn't been here, but tonight, they were – no doubt as a result of the inspector's instructions that nobody was to leave the hotel.

Without names, ages or nationalities, I was almost completely in the dark. If it really had been murder, any one of our fellow diners could have hit a seriously drunk man over the head and tipped his body off the cliff – or even just given him a shove. The key to discovering the identity of the murderer had to be motive. Why had Graziani been targeted? What did we know about the victim, apart from the fact that he'd done some terrible things two decades ago and had subsequently been locked up in prison until only a month ago? It seemed logical to assume that his death might in some way be connected with the crimes he'd committed long ago but, of course, other reasons could also exist. I would dearly have liked to know more about the man, but this information would be on the Italian police computer system and not available to me.

Or would it?

I pulled out my phone and walked down into the garden, out of earshot of any of the guests, and called Marco Innocenti in Florence. I had first met Marco when he had been Sergeant Innocenti, Virgilio's right-hand man, and he had since been promoted to inspector. I knew him well by now and trusted him implicitly as a capable police officer and friend, and I felt confident that he trusted me. He and Virgilio had always had a close working relationship, and I felt sure he would be only too keen to help his boss. He answered almost immediately.

'*Ciao*, Dan. How's Elba?'

'*Ciao*, Marco. It's a beautiful island. I'm not interrupting your dinner, am I? Listen, we have a situation here and we need your help.'

'Of course, what's happened?' He sounded intrigued.

'Does the name Ignazio Graziani mean anything to you? From about twenty years ago.'

'Graziani... no, I can't say it does. Mind you, twenty years ago, I was still in short trousers.' This was an exaggeration, but it didn't surprise me that the name was unfamiliar to him.

'He was sent down for twenty-five years for multiple cases of kidnap and aggravated rape – in or around Pisa, I believe.'

'The *commissario* would be able to help you there, Dan. He used to work out of Pisa.'

'That's the problem, Marco – Virgilio certainly did know Graziani.' I went on to outline the events of the last twenty-four hours, culminating in

Virgilio being escorted to the local police station for questioning. Marco sounded understandably shocked.

'They've arrested the boss? For murder?'

'No, they're just questioning him at the moment, but there's quite a lot of circumstantial evidence that isn't going to help his case. What I want to do is to help him any way I can, and what I'm hoping you can do is to find out as much as possible about Ignazio Graziani. I believe he's originally from the island of Elba, so names and addresses of friends and relatives would be good. Also if you can find out as much as possible about his victims, that would be very helpful.'

'Of course. I'll get onto it straight away. Assuming it wasn't the boss – and we both know it can't have been him – are there any other suspects?'

'At the moment, it looks likely that the murderer – assuming that it was murder, and that's by no means definite – is somebody here in this hotel. The good news is that the place is only half-full so that probably narrows it down to about a dozen people.'

'Give me their names and I'll do a bit of digging. It's the least I can do for the boss.'

'I don't have names at the moment but I'm hoping to be able to get them from the receptionist. I'll do what I can and I'll e-mail you what I find out.'

When the conversation ended, I returned to Anna and Lina. 'Marco's on the case. Between us, we'll find out what really happened. Don't you worry.'

Neither of them looked convinced, and I didn't blame them. All I could do for now was hope I was right.

8

SUNDAY NIGHT

As soon as I finished my coffee, I went through to Reception, where I found Rita sipping a coffee on her own. She looked up and produced a little smile as she recognised me. I could see that it was a struggle, but dead bodies do tend to cast a shadow over people.

'Signor Armstrong, how are you? I hope the terrible events of last night haven't spoilt your holiday. We're so sorry.'

'It's not your fault, Rita, and please call me Dan. I'm afraid we have a big problem.' I went on to tell her the latest developments without going into detail about Virgilio's confrontation with the murdered man last night. When I told her that he had been marched off to the police station to be questioned, she looked predictably horrified.

'They think it was murder? I don't believe that for a moment. Besides, Virgilio wouldn't hurt a fly. He's a police officer, and a high-ranking one. There's no way he's a killer.'

In fact, I had come across several police officers in my time who had turned out to be murderers – one here in Italy – but I wisely decided not to mention this to her. The good news was that it looked as though she was firmly on team Virgilio, so I outlined what I was hoping to get from her.

'I don't know if Virgilio told you, but I used to be a police officer in the UK and I now have my own investigation agency in Florence. I'm determined to give Virgilio all the help I can, but what I really need is some information from you.'

'Anything, just say the word.' She leant forward and lowered her voice. 'The police inspector sounded as though he thought it was just an accident, but if it turns out to have been murder, do you think it might be somebody here who did it?' Her eyes flitted across to the door to the owner's office. 'Signor Silvano won't like it if the police start interrogating the guests, but I suppose that would be the logical assumption. You and I both know it wasn't Virgilio, so who do you think it was?'

'That's what I'm hoping to find out. There are two things I'd like from you. If possible, could you show me or tell me where the CCTV cameras are situated and, more importantly, could you give me a list of the names and details of the staff and guests here at the hotel?'

I waited anxiously for her to say no, but I needn't have worried.

'Of course. I can let you have a copy of everybody on the payroll and all the guests' names if you give me your e-mail address. I've had to send all these to the police so it won't take me long. As well as the guests' names, I'll send you over the copies of all their ID documents – but you'd probably best not mention that to the inspector.'

Hotels in Italy are obliged by law to keep a record of all guests, and I had been hoping I might get sight of their documents. I thanked her warmly and promised I wouldn't reveal the extent of her help. I gave her my e-mail and she told me she would get onto it straight away, but she hadn't finished yet.

'Now, as far as the CCTV's concerned, why don't I show you what's on the screen?' She pressed a couple of keys on the keyboard and swung the monitor around so we could both see it. It was immediately clear that the hotel had four cameras, one here in the reception area and the other three outside. The inside one didn't interest me for now, but I studied the external ones carefully. One covered the terrace, one the parking area, and the last the front door and the path leading towards the clifftop and, beyond it, the beach. Filing away the fact that last night's confrontation with Graziani at our table would definitely have been recorded and had probably already been noted by the police, I concentrated on camera number four. This was the one looking out towards the beach.

The screen showed the gravel path leading from the villa in the direction of the sea. Frustratingly, it disappeared into the pine trees, but at least that meant that the camera hadn't been able to pick up the spot where Virgilio had punched Graziani. The clifftop directly above the dead body, presumably where the man had either jumped, fallen or been pushed over the cliff edge, was hidden by trees, which disappeared from sight at the edge of the field of vision of the camera. On this basis, it would have been easy for somebody here at the hotel – assuming they could find a way of avoiding the camera at the front door – to sneak into these trees and gain access to the cliffs without being seen.

Clearly, CCTV wasn't going to be much help. The only good news was that it wasn't likely to provide the police with any hard evidence to use against Virgilio, either.

I thanked Rita most warmly and went back out to the terrace where Anna and Lina were still at the table. Some of the other guests had already finished their dinner and left, and only three other tables were now occupied: by the two people who had dined with Graziani the previous night, the amorous young couple at the far end of the terrace, and the two hard nuts. I studied these two closely, if surreptitiously.

The one with the ginger hair was leaning across the table, saying something to the man sitting opposite him. From the expressions on their faces, whatever he was saying, they were both taking it seriously. They were too far away for me to be able to make out what was being said, but from the hand gestures and the movements of the lips, it looked to me as though they were Italian. There were some documents on the table between them and the man with the ginger hair was tapping a sheet with his finger, clearly making a point. The one with the shaved head was nodding sagely. I had the feeling they were here on business and I wondered what sort of business that might be. After a glance at their watches, both men stood up, collected the documents and headed back into the hotel.

The amorous couple at the end of the terrace were still lost in each other's eyes and looked as if they would be happy to stay there all night. I did my best to take a closer look at the two people on Graziani's table but it was fully dark by now and the candlelight didn't help much. Graziani had allegedly been almost fifty, and the man sitting there was probably around the same age, although I could only see him in profile, while the candle was closer to his female companion and she looked a lot younger, maybe in her thirties or even late twenties. The man was smartly dressed in a polo shirt and he was smoking a cigar, whose aroma floated down on the slight hint of a breeze in the evening air as far as our table. Neither of them appeared to be speaking. Then, without preamble, the man got to his feet and headed back into the hotel, immediately followed by his female companion. As they disappeared from sight, I found myself wondering what sort of relationship they had. Was he maybe her boss? Was she his mistress or trophy wife? Was she his daughter? Hopefully, when Rita sent me their IDs, the mystery would be explained.

I was roused from any further conjecture by the sound of a phone. It was Virgilio calling Lina, telling her the inspector had finished with him and asking her to drive over and pick him up from Portoferraio. When the call finished and she explained what he had just said, I waved her back into her seat and told her I'd go. This wasn't just natural chivalry – if you asked my ex-wife, she would probably tell you that this was never one of my strong points, although I've been trying harder as I grow older – but it was so that I could discuss the case with him before returning him to the welcoming arms of his wife.

The drive from the hotel on the east coast of the island to Portoferraio on the north coast took barely fifteen minutes and I got there at nine-thirty. Elba isn't big. It's barely twenty miles long, and at this time of night, the roads were wonderfully clear of traffic. The police station was close to the ferry terminal through which we had arrived on the island and I found Virgilio waiting by the main door. I waved to him and he climbed into my van alongside me.

'*Ciao*, Dan, this is very good of you.' He sounded tired.

'No problem, how're you doing?'

He ran a weary hand over his shaved head. 'I've almost lost my voice. I've had to repeat my story to Bellini, to his boss, and even via video link to the *Questore* himself over on the mainland in Livorno.'

'Wow, the big guns.' I was impressed but not surprised – after all, news of an officer at chief inspector level potentially involved in a murder was bound to go all the way up the chain of command to the *Questore* – roughly equivalent to the chief constable back in the UK – and had to be handled very tactfully, starting with making sure the media didn't get so much as a whiff of it. As it turned out, this contact had been good for Virgilio as he explained.

'Actually, that was no bad thing for me. I know the *Questore* pretty well. He was my super when I was starting out in Pisa. He remembered me – for all the right reasons – and he personally instructed Bellini to release me.'

'So you're a free man.'

'Sort of, but, like you and the other guests, I have to stay at the hotel until we get permission to leave, but Bellini left me in no doubt that, if it turns out to have been murder – although I'm convinced he still believes it was an accident – I'm the prime suspect as far as he's concerned.' He shrugged. 'And I can't blame him. Who else is there?'

'With cousin Rita's help, that's what we need to find out. Mind you, I would have thought Bellini might have got somebody to give you a lift back to the hotel.'

'I think he was making a point, telling me not to expect any favours from him just because I'm a police officer.'

As I drove out of town, I related what I'd discovered from the CCTV footage, and he nodded.

'I thought the CCTV imagery would prove interesting. It was the scene with Graziani at our table last night that put Bellini onto me. That and the cameras picking me up walking back through the trees to the hotel after eleven, only ten minutes or so after Graziani had lurched out along the path into the trees.'

'Did the CCTV show anybody else walking around at that time of night?'

'Not that he told me. He was keeping his cards very close to his chest but, again, I don't blame him for that.'

I braked hard as a scrawny, black and white cat shot across the road in front of me. 'But the fact is that nobody knows for sure whether it was accident, suicide or murder. Unless they find a murder weapon, I could see the whole case being closed down by this time tomorrow, couldn't you?'

There was a pause before Virgilio replied. 'Whatever Inspector Bellini thinks, something tells me it was murder, Dan. One thing's for sure:

Graziani didn't commit suicide. He's not the type. If he were going to take his own life out of some sort of excess of guilt, surely he would have done it years ago in prison. I suppose an accident is possible – he was seriously drunk, after all – but there's something telling me that we're looking at a murder. I've been thinking back on last night and the more I think about it, the more I'm convinced there was somebody else out there on the clifftop when I had my confrontation with Graziani.'

'Did you see anybody?'

'Nothing definite, but for a second, I thought there might have been a movement in the shadows of the trees. At the time, I was so hyped up after smacking Graziani that I dismissed it as my imagination or some random animal and headed back to the hotel.'

We were out of town by this time and the road curled upwards over the hill towards the east coast. As we climbed, I reflected on what he had just said and realised that I tended to agree with him.

'Whether you saw somebody or not, you could well be right about it being murder. Certainly, Graziani must have had a lot of enemies after what he did to those women. Twenty years is a long time to wait for revenge, but with him locked up in prison, now is just about the first opportunity anybody could have had to kill him. The biggest problem with that scenario, as I see it, is how did a potential murderer know that Graziani was going to be here at this hotel right now? That implies local knowledge or close surveillance, doesn't it?'

'Definitely. The killer must have known that he was going to be here last night, which is unlikely, so I can see why the inspector thinks it was a simple drunken accident. But if it turns out to have been murder, as you and I believe, the perpetrator almost certainly has to be somebody here at the hotel.'

'The question is, who?'

9

SUNDAY NIGHT/MONDAY MORNING

When I got back to the room just before ten and picked up my laptop, I found that Rita had been true to her word and had sent me a load of information. I settled down and eagerly studied the details. Beside me, Anna was once more engrossed in her historical tome, but she took time out from her studies to shoot me an enquiring look.

'I suppose this means that you're going to have to revert to being a detective again.' Before I could attempt an apology, she reached over and tapped me gently on the back of the hand. 'Don't worry, I'm not going to moan at you. You have no choice, I get that. This is your best friend we're talking about, after all. Personally, judging from the state that Graziani was in last night, it wouldn't surprise me in the slightest if his death were accidental, but I quite understand that you need to do everything you can to help Virgilio.'

I breathed a sigh of relief. 'Thanks, Anna. It's like you say: I have no choice. I owe it to Virgilio to help any way I can to clear him of suspicion. Still, I promise it isn't going to occupy me twenty-four hours a day and I'm still up for our windsurfing lesson tomorrow.'

'You're sure about the windsurfing?'

'Yes, genuinely. I think I might be beginning to get the hang of it, even if

I'm sure I can hear the water in my ears – or maybe my brain – swilling around as I move my head.'

She returned to her medieval studies and I started looking through the wealth of information Rita had sent me. I spent almost an hour sifting through the documents and soon realised that there was one important omission: there was no mention of the man and the woman who had dined with the victim the previous night. This confirmed that they weren't guests at the hotel, but the fact that I had seen them again this evening made me think that they were almost certainly living locally. Whether this meant that they were residents of the island or just here on holiday remained to be seen, but as they had known the victim, they were significant. I resolved to speak to Rita in the morning in the hope that she might be able to shed some light on their identity.

As far as the others were concerned, I gradually sifted them into two camps: 'likely' and 'unlikely'. Into the unlikely camp, I put Tatsuo Tanaka, the four Brits, Heidi Engadin and Martin Wolf from Zurich, along with the couple of young lovers. They both shared the surname, Arnaldo, and Monica had added a note indicating that this was their honeymoon. I tended to discount the foreign guests because I felt convinced that this murder had a local, or at least a Tuscan, dimension. My feeling was that the young honeymooners probably had other things on their minds rather than committing murder, but I knew that they would have to be checked all the same. Leaving them aside for now, this left me with the two hard nuts and the couple from the beach on the first day, so I concentrated on the two tough guys first.

Rita had sent me copies of their documents, and I saw that the ginger-haired one was called Filippo Guerra, age thirty-seven, resident in Rome, while the one with the shaved head was Carlo Donati, also from Rome – but a different address – and he was a year older. The other couple were Fernando Giardino and his wife, Erica. He was the man we had seen running up the path from the beach the previous afternoon and he was almost exactly the same age as me, just about to turn fifty-eight, while his wife was two years older. They both lived in Lucca, two or three hours away from here.

Before taking Oscar for his late-night walk, I sent the details of all four

to Marco in Florence so he could run them through the police computer
system.

* * *

At seven next morning, when I went out with Oscar, there were already two
police cars and a minivan in the car park, and tape blocking off the path to
the beach. A team of police officers were combing through the trees on the
clifftop and an orange rigid inflatable boat was down by the beach with
people in wetsuits clearly getting ready to search the seabed for the murder
weapon. I wished the constable on duty at the top of the path good luck,
but I had a feeling it was a forlorn hope. And without a murder weapon, I
had little doubt that the inspector would decide to leave it at that and put
Graziani's death down to either misadventure or suicide.

After breakfast with the others, Virgilio and I sat down in his room to
go through what we had so far. Marco had managed to access the original
Graziani file and had produced an excellent summary of the main find-
ings. We studied it carefully, making a note of the names of the four
victims and cross-checking them against the names of the guests here at
the hotel. None of them matched, making it less likely – but not impossible – that somebody here had been related to them and had deliberately
come here out for revenge. There was also the problem of how such a
person could have discovered that the victim was going to be here. All of
Graziani's four victims had lived in or near Pisa, which was over a hundred
kilometres from the island, and I had a hunch that the murderer – if
indeed there were one – would be found here on Elba. After all, I imagined
it would have been common knowledge that when Graziani had been
released from jail he would, in all probability, have returned to his home
turf.

I studied the photos of the four victims and it was immediately clear
that Graziani had gone out of his way to pick attractive young women. All
four had been in their early twenties and they all had dark hair. According
to the file, Graziani had stalked each of them for days or weeks before
carrying out his assaults. Three had been students at the *Scuola Normale
Superiore di Pisa* – one of Italy's top universities – and the other had been a

librarian working at the university. I could only begin to imagine the horrors they had endured at his hands.

At just after nine, we got another e-mail from Marco that made interesting reading. Mr and Mrs Giardino from Lucca had received a clean bill of health – they would appear to be harmless shopkeepers – but the two tough guys had both popped up on the police system, though not with criminal records. It turned out that they were *Carabinieri* officers belonging to the TPC. I was unfamiliar with the acronym and Virgilio explained.

'TPC stands for the *Comando Carabinieri Tutela Patrimonio Culturale* – the *Carabinieri* art squad. I've worked with them a few times, most recently three years back when they uncovered a flourishing gang of forgers working out of Florence, producing convincing-looking fake old masters.' He looked up and shot me a wink. 'The TPC are pretty good... for *Carabinieri*.'

I couldn't help smiling at his grudging admiration. Italy has a dizzying array of different police forces, ranging from the *Polizia*, the state police of which Virgilio was an officer, to the *Carabinieri*, who started life as a branch of the army and now operate to a great extent in parallel with the *Polizia*. Along with them are separate branches specialising in financial matters, illegal immigration and road traffic – to name just a few. Since settling here in Italy, I had occasionally worked with both the police and the *Carabinieri* and had often questioned how they managed to collaborate without overlapping or competing. I wondered whether these two guys were here on holiday or on duty. And if they were here for work, what might have brought them to the island?

Either way, the knowledge that these two were on the side of law and order came as a bit of a disappointment. I had definitely been considering them as potential murderers – mainly based on their hard physical appearance – but it now seemed that I had been wrong and had misjudged them. Yes, they could still be killers, but it was less likely. I had to smile when I imagined Inspector Bellini's frustration at finding himself faced with three serving Italian police officers and one former British copper among the suspects. As I knew from experience, police officers are some of the most difficult people to interview, mainly because they're so used to asking the very same questions.

Virgilio and I talked through the other suspects, including the owner and staff of the hotel. On Saturday evening, there had been seven people working here: Rita in Reception, the chef, an assistant chef, a waiter, a waitress, the night porter and Signor Silvano, the owner. The kitchen and serving staff had all left at ten along with Rita, and Signor Silvano had retired to his private apartment on the top floor shortly afterwards. This left the night porter as the only staff member actually here at the time of Graziani's death. No doubt the inspector's people would already have interviewed the staff, but as we were not part of the investigation, we had not been given access to the results.

It was possible that one of the foreigners might turn out to have a suspicious past, but I wasn't holding my breath. I was still convinced that the murderer was to be found far closer to home here on the island.

Rousing Oscar from the floor at my feet, Virgilio and I went downstairs to Reception, where we found Rita. She gave Virgilio a concerned look when she saw him.

'*Ciao*, Virgilio, how did it go with the police last night?'

He gave her a smile in return. 'As you can see, I'm a free man. They still don't know whether it was an accident, suicide or murder, but you probably know that they're doing a fingertip search among the trees on the clifftop. They've also got divers in the water looking for a possible murder weapon, but Dan and I tend to think that they're unlikely to come up with anything.'

'So you think it wasn't murder after all? That's what I think.' She sounded quite convinced. 'I've been looking at some of the CCTV footage on Saturday night, and the victim looked as though he was blind drunk – and the serving staff confirm that. I reckon he just fell over the cliff edge in the dark. It's easily done.'

Virgilio gave a guarded reply. 'I'm not sure whether it was an accident or something more, but you're right, Graziani was certainly drunk, and he might easily have fallen. That seems to be what the inspector thinks. I imagine that if the police don't find anything significant today, Inspector Bellini will probably call it an accident and leave it at that. Tell me, did you know the victim? Was he a regular here and who were his dinner companions – a man and a younger woman?'

She hesitated before replying. 'I wasn't familiar with the man who died, but I know who he was. His brother, Aldo, comes here now and then.' She glanced across at me. 'You've been doing a windsurfing course, haven't you, Dan? Aldo Graziani owns the windsurfing academy, as well as the campsite behind the beach. There's quite a good pizzeria there, but Aldo likes his food, and our restaurant is a step up from the pizzeria.'

Virgilio and I exchanged glances. So the two men had been brothers. This was very interesting. Virgilio took up the questions again. 'And the young woman who was with them on Saturday and who was here last night with Aldo Graziani, who's she?'

'Her name's Teresa, but I'm afraid I don't know her other name. She works for Aldo. She often comes in with him and some of us have been wondering whether there might be something going on between them – even though she's much younger than he is.'

'What about the man who died, Ignazio Graziani? Was he staying with his brother?'

Again, there was a momentary hesitation from Rita. 'I believe so.' She paused. 'I imagine you know where he's been for the past twenty years and why.' There was clear revulsion in her voice.

Virgilio nodded. 'Yes, indeed. What about other people around here? Did they know what he'd done?'

Her reply was uncompromising. 'Everybody knew. It's been the talk of Santa Sabina for the last month, and I heard that some people are thinking of organising a petition to get him to move away.'

This was also potentially interesting. If the victim had been universally hated by the locals, maybe there had been somebody who had decided to take direct action. I queried Ignazio's relationship with his brother.

'Assuming he was staying with his brother, was that because they were close?'

'I very much doubt it. You can imagine the shame he brought on the family.'

I could imagine that only too well. 'And yet his brother still took him back?'

'That's what it looks like, but I'm quite sure it was under duress.

Presumably, Ignazio had nowhere else to go, and Aldo felt he had no choice.' She caught my eye. 'Mind you, Aldo's no saint himself.'

'Does he have a wife, family?'

'He was married, but his wife divorced him and moved away years ago. As far as I know, they didn't have any children.'

'And does he live at the campsite?'

'Aldo lives in the villa on the little hill behind the beach. He inherited some land and a little campsite from his father, who died five or six years ago, and since then, he's bought more land, quadrupled the size of the campsite, opened the windsurfing academy and built the villa – we call it Villa Ostentatious. You should see it – talk about a modern monstrosity! God knows how he got planning permission – it sticks out like a sore thumb. I don't like that sort of thing myself, but there's no accounting for taste, is there?'

Virgilio thanked Rita and he and I went out. There wasn't a cloud in the sky, and the sun was already scorching hot. I reminded myself that I would need to slap on some sunscreen before my windsurfing lesson. As soon as we were out of range of anybody, we stopped in the shade of a big umbrella pine to discuss what we'd just heard. Something Rita had said had struck both of us as potentially significant and Virgilio voiced it first.

'If Aldo Graziani inherited the land from his father then, according to Italian law, Ignazio must also have inherited a share. I wonder whether we've just found a motive for murder. How about this? Aldo is making a good living here while his brother languishes in prison. Then the prodigal son reappears and wants to claim his share. Maybe Aldo didn't feel like sharing and he came up with the solution of taking his brother out for dinner, making sure he consumed a few bottles of wine, and then pushed him off the clifftop.'

'The same thought's been going through my head. When I go to the windsurfing beach later on to have my lesson, I'll do a little bit of asking around. Ideally, it would be good to sit down and interview Aldo as well as the woman, Teresa.' I gave a frustrated hiss. 'If only we were the investigating officers, but of course, I'm nothing to do with it, and you're outside your jurisdiction. Are you going to mention this to Inspector Bellini as a hypothesis?'

'Let's see if his people come up with a murder weapon first but, yes, he needs to know. Of course, if he's been doing his job properly, I would hope he would already have this information, so it could be that he's already spoken to Aldo. I'm not holding my breath, though, because it's pretty clear to me that Bellini's still convinced it was an accident. Please do keep your ears open, and I'll sit down and call Marco in Florence to see if, between us, we can dig a little deeper into what happened twenty years ago. It had a powerful and lasting effect on me, but it's not as though the victims were members of my family. I can only imagine the grief and the anger felt by the women themselves and their nearest and dearest. Yes, Aldo, the brother, might be our man, but I still think Ignazio Graziani's death could be a revenge killing, relating to the terrible things he did all those years ago. I'll come along and join you after lunch, ostensibly to watch you falling in the water again, but mostly to see if I can chat to a few people there who know the background to the family.'

'It was interesting to hear that the locals are up in arms about Ignazio coming back here. It sounds as though tempers have been running high.'

'And creating a potentially very embarrassing situation for his brother. Apart from the question of the inheritance, I imagine that Aldo can't have been best pleased when his jailbird brother reappeared – especially as Rita says that what he'd done was common knowledge around here.' He gave me a knowing look. 'Another reason for doing away with him maybe?'

'Yes, indeed.' I changed the subject. 'What about our two *Carabinieri* friends? Do we talk to them?'

'Let's wait and see if a murder weapon turns up first – and if it really was murder.' He looked across at me with a funny expression on his face. 'I'll be completely honest with you, Dan: I'm glad Graziani's dead, and part of me would be more than happy to see his death dismissed as an unfortunate accident, and that's that. If it turns out to have been murder, I'm not saying I applaud anybody taking the law into their own hands, but there's a part of me, and I acknowledge that it's a very unprofessional part of me, that genuinely believes the murderer did the world a favour.'

I didn't answer. What he said was totally contrary to everything I'd been taught in my years at the Met, but I could see where he was coming from. In his eyes, justice had been done but, deep down, I wasn't so sure. My mother used to say that two wrongs never made a right. If there was a murderer out there, was it really right to leave them unpunished?

10

MONDAY MORNING

Oscar and I went for a walk after breakfast. First, I wanted to satisfy my curiosity and I headed for the coast. I managed to find a spot further along the clifftop from where I could look back onto the beach and see what progress, if any, the police were making as they searched the seabed. It was a delightful morning and I was relieved to find that there was very little wind. As far as my stuttering windsurfing career was concerned, all I felt able to handle at the moment was a gentle breeze at best. Looking down from above, I could see not only the people on the beach but also the shapes of the divers underwater. One of the most stunning facets of the island of Elba is how clean and unpolluted the waters around it are. For somebody used to the murky waters of the River Thames, it made a very welcome change.

I threw sticks for Oscar to retrieve – inland, away from the cliff edge – while I perched on a rocky outcrop and observed developments below me. As I sat there, my thoughts returned yet again to the murder mystery I was trying to write. In a way, I was faced with the same problem in my book as here in real life. Just like the body at the foot of the tower in San Gimignano, was this death accidental or self-inflicted, or had a murderer been at work? The more I thought about it, the more I hoped that solving one mystery might help me solve the other.

After sitting there for about five minutes, I had to admit that I was no closer to breaking out of my writer's block, and it became clear to me that nothing of note was happening here at the beach, so Oscar and I resumed our walk. This time, I headed inland to check out the village of Santa Sabina sull'Elba, and it turned out to be even smaller than I had imagined.

It took barely five minutes to walk from one end of the village to the other, and as far as I could see, there were only half a dozen narrow streets and not more than a hundred houses in the whole place. The centre was clearly the little piazza in front of the church where there was a single *alimentari* shop, advertising everything from ice cream to firewood. Alongside it was the Bar del Centro with half a dozen tables outside on the grey flagstones, only one of them currently occupied. The occupants were two elderly gentlemen whose wrinkled skin had been burnt a deep walnut colour by the sun, and it was plain that they had spent most, if not all, of their lives outdoors. They didn't look like tourists, so I took a chance on them being locals prepared to talk and sat down at a table nearby.

Oscar wandered over to greet them, his tail wagging good-naturedly, and one of the men rewarded him with a pat on the back. A waiter appeared through the beaded fly curtain at the door of the bar and asked me what I'd like, so I decided to have an espresso and settled back in the shade cast by the bulk of the church across the square from us. When the waiter returned, he stopped to chat.

'I haven't seen you around. Are you here on holiday?'

'Yes, I'm taking a week off. I live and work just outside Florence.'

He subjected me to closer scrutiny. 'From your accent, you're not from around here. Sounds to me like you're from the north, maybe Trentino?'

I gave him a smile. 'Further north than that. I'm English but I've been living and working here now for a few years. What about you? Are you a local?'

He nodded. 'Born and bred.'

I took advantage of his willingness to chat and did a little bit of digging – even if I already knew the answer to my opening question, thanks to Rita. 'Can you satisfy my curiosity? I've been doing a course at the windsurfing academy on the beach. Who does that belong to?'

'The windsurfing school is owned by the same person who owns the campsite behind the beach. His name's Graziani, Aldo Graziani.'

I did my best to feign ignorance. 'I recognise that name. Is he related to that poor man who fell off the cliff, by any chance?'

For the first time, one of the elderly men on the next table joined in. '*Poor man?* Don't waste any sympathy on scum like that. He was evil to the core.'

Still doing my best to look clueless, I queried his comment. 'In what way? What did he do that was so evil?'

The old man gave a theatrical shudder. 'I couldn't even begin to tell you, but he was bad news, and we're all better off without him.'

The other elderly man added a comment of his own. 'We booted him off the island twenty years ago and we were getting ready to do the same again. We don't want his sort here.'

This was new. Still doing my best to sound casual, I queried what he had said. 'Booted out, in what way?'

A sour look appeared on the old man's face. 'Back then, he made a pest of himself with the local women and girls – some of them still in their teens. They say he even tried to abduct a girl here, and if she hadn't managed to jump out of his van and escape before he could drive off with her, who knows what might have happened?'

'Did she go to the police?'

He shook his head and the waiter added a few words of explanation. 'To be honest, that's just hearsay – a rumour that's been going around for so long that people believe it even though there's no proof. Nobody knows whether the attempted abduction really took place but, even if it wasn't true, by that time, everybody was sick and tired of Ignazio and something needed to be done.'

The elderly man picked up the tale again. 'A bunch of us went around to his home one evening and spoke to Tommaso, his father, in no uncertain terms. Either Ignazio left the island for good, or we would report him to the police.'

I very nearly told him that if they had reported Graziani to the police, maybe those four girls in Pisa would never have been assaulted, but I bit my tongue and stayed silent. Instead, I nodded slowly and continued to press for more information. 'And he left?'

'He had no choice. His father threw him out of the house – old Tommaso was no fool; he knew what Ignazio was like. With nowhere to live and with no friends, Ignazio left the island to start a new life in Pisa.'

I didn't mention the man's criminal record and just asked what he'd gone off to do in Pisa, but the barman didn't mince his words. 'He did some really bad stuff in Pisa and he's been in prison for twenty years. He came crawling back a few weeks ago.'

'To get his share of his inheritance.' The other elderly man picked up the story. 'And his brother must be rejoicing now that he's dead. Aldo's built up a good business. The last thing he needed was to share it with that pervert.'

'Mind you, Aldo isn't much better.' The barista was frowning and I gave him an enquiring look. After a few moments' hesitation, he explained. 'I don't mean he's a perverted sadist like his brother, but he's got an awful reputation here as far as women are concerned.'

One of the elderly men joined in. 'And that includes married women as well. He doesn't come into town any more, he just stays in that flashy villa of his, and that's probably very wise. If he did show his face here, he would almost certainly find himself on the receiving end of a beating.'

Before I could ask for any more detail, a pair of elderly women appeared and sat down at a nearby table. I saw the three men exchange glances and the conversation instantly changed to football – always a fertile topic. I wondered who the women were. Were they just nosey locals or might there have been a connection with the Graziani family? Either way, it was clear that I wasn't going to get any more information, so I swallowed my coffee, paid the waiter, and set off towards the hotel.

All the way back, I was turning over in my head what I'd just heard. Clearly, the Graziani brothers hadn't been held in high esteem by a lot of the locals, and the story of the attempted abduction was potentially fascinating – if it was true. Maybe the girl or her close family had decided to get their revenge. The list of possible perpetrators was expanding.

* * *

Back at the hotel, the police vehicles were still parked outside, and I could see figures moving among the pine trees, but somehow. I had a feeling that by this evening, the death of Ignazio Graziani could well be written off as an unfortunate accident – and, indeed, in the absence of any proof to the contrary, that's what it might have been, in spite of the growing list of people who had wanted him dead.

Anna and I went around to the windsurfing beach at ten-thirty, and I found a helpful volunteer in the shape of the waiter at the beach bar who said he would make sure he kept an eye on Oscar while the two of us were out in the water. I tied the lead to one of the supports of the awning in front of the bar, told him to be a good boy, and off we went. He's normally pretty good about staying put when I tell him, but I could see the sense of injustice written across his face when he saw us heading for the water while he was obliged to stay on dry land. I vowed to make sure I gave him a good long splash about in the waves as soon as the first half of my lesson finished.

The lesson itself went a whole lot better than the previous day. Yes, I still fell in quite a few times, but I definitely felt more confident, and by lunchtime, I was really getting the hang of tilting the sail so that it could catch the wind and drive me along. When I carried my board back up the beach and set it down, Ingrid told me ominously that this afternoon would be devoted to 'tacking' and 'gybing'. Helpfully, she used the English words, but they didn't really mean much to me. I have to confess that I had to look them up on my phone and saw that these manoeuvres would involve 'changing course by turning into and through the wind' or, alternatively, 'making a downwind turn so that the sail crosses to the leeward side of the boat'. This left me little the wiser, but I had a feeling that the result of this would be more falling in.

I found Oscar pleased to see me with a contented canine smile on his face that was quickly explained by the waiter, who told me a group of kids had come in for mid-morning cakes and croissants and Oscar had scored numerous titbits as a result. Consequently, although I would happily have slumped into a chair and stayed there for the next hour and a half, I swallowed half a litre of water – not seawater for a change – and set off to give him a bit of exercise, leaving Anna relating our windsurfing experiences to her daughter on the phone.

I gave Oscar a quick, refreshing swim and then, out of curiosity, I headed inland, following the signs to the *campeggio*. According to what I'd been told, presumably this was now wholly owned by the victim's brother, Aldo, unless Ignazio had made other provisions in his will. As far as I was aware, this was unlikely as Ignazio hadn't been married, had no children, and his parents had died some years earlier. As I walked past rows of tents, smart-looking timber chalets, tennis courts, a large swimming pool, and all the facilities of a modern campsite, it occurred to me yet again that this might indeed have been a motive for fratricide. There could be no doubt that Aldo Graziani had benefited considerably from his brother's death.

I walked through the campsite and out the other side to find myself close to the main road, just along from a sign indicating the entrance to Hotel Augustus. An immaculately trimmed hedge enclosed a little hillock on which I could see Aldo Graziani's villa. As Rita had said, the 'Villa Ostentatious' was an ultramodern building with white walls, acres of plate glass and a flat roof. It was in an enviable position and it was no doubt worth a lot of money. I was struck yet again by how well Aldo had done for himself – maybe suspiciously well?

I turned back into the campsite and decided that it wouldn't do any harm to sit down at the bar and have a drink in the hope of maybe finding out a bit more about the owner of this place. The sign above the door said *Bar/Pizzeria* and people were sitting at tables outside, enjoying their lunch. I had promised Anna that I would eat with her at the beach bar so, much to Oscar's chagrin – he has a thing about pizza crusts – I attracted the attention of a passing waiter and just asked if I could have a low-alcohol beer. He waved me into a seat on the terrace and went off to get my drink.

While waiting, I turned over in my head the fact that Ignazio's brother had had good motive to kill. I wondered whether maybe in my book, I should introduce a brother or other friend or relative who might have pushed the victim off the top of the San Gimignano tower. After all, he had pretty obviously gone up the tower willingly, so that did tend to imply that if he'd been in the company of the murderer, he would already have been familiar with him or her. As far as motive was concerned, it wouldn't be hard for me to invent an oil well in Texas or an IT company in Silicon Valley and a jealous or greedy relative. It occurred to me that I needed to think very carefully about the terms of the dead man's will, and I felt a little spurt of inspiration run through me. There might be light at the end of the tunnel as far as my fictitious murders were concerned after all.

When the waiter returned, he also very kindly brought a bowl of water for Oscar, who slurped it up willingly. The waiter was friendly, probably around my age, and I took the opportunity to ask him a few questions, starting with the same ploy I'd used before.

'I'm doing a windsurfing course down at the academy on the beach. Does that belong to the campsite as well?'

He nodded. 'Yes, it's all part of the Graziani empire.'

'Does that mean that the owner's a wealthy man?'

He gave me a rueful wink. 'Put it this way: he's a whole lot richer than I am.'

'Have you worked here long?'

'Ever since I had to give up farming. That's five years ago now.'

'You had to give it up. Was there a problem?'

His smiley face became more serious. 'It's hard to work in the fields when there are no fields to work in.' In response to my questioning look, he explained. 'I used to work for Ernesto Morso. He owned vineyards in the fields around here, some of which have now been turned into the new campsite.' He gestured at the buildings around him. 'That's when all this development took place. Before that, it was just a small campsite for a couple of dozen tents. Just look at it now.'

'So the farmer decided to sell the land and you were out of a job?'

'It wasn't so much that he decided to sell, but that he had no option but to sell.' He glanced around more furtively now. 'Aldo's a tough business-man. He knows how to get what he wants.'

I filed this piece of information away for future reference. If Aldo Graziani's business methods were questionable, might that have been a reason why somebody had tried to kill *him*, but in the dark, had only succeeded in killing his brother? If it was true that Ernesto Morso had somehow been forced to sell his land to Graziani against his will, why might this have been? This sounded very much like blackmail to me and I knew that Ernesto Morso deserved to be investigated. I gave the waiter a sympathetic smile.

'At least waiting at table is an easier job – hopefully.'

He didn't respond to my comment. Instead, he very conveniently brought the subject around to Aldo Graziani's dead brother. 'Aldo's a lucky, lucky man.' From the way he said it, I got the feeling he had reservations about how much good fortune Aldo Graziani deserved. 'You probably don't know this, but he's just inherited the whole thing. His brother died a couple of nights ago, and that makes Aldo even richer than he was before.'

I decided to feign ignorance once more. 'That sounds very convenient. How did his brother die?'

'He got drunk and fell off the cliff – or so they say.' He glanced around cautiously once more before continuing. 'A bit *too* convenient if you ask me.' Realising that he was talking about his boss to a complete stranger, he straightened up and glanced back towards the entrance. 'But what do I know? I'm just a waiter these days. I've seen the police cars up at the hotel, so maybe they'll get to the bottom of it.' He turned and disappeared back into the café, leaving me to reflect on what I'd heard.

There could be no doubt that, just as the men at the village bar had said, Ignazio Graziani's death had indeed been very convenient for his brother. In a matter of a few seconds, the rightful claimant to half of Aldo's empire had been eliminated. I had known people murdered for far less. And now there was Ernesto Morso. Might he have borne a grudge against the man who had forced him to sell up – maybe by dubious means? If I'd been the investigating officer – and I had to remind myself firmly that I wasn't – I would be adding Aldo Graziani and Ernesto Morso to the list of suspects. If Ignazio hadn't been murdered by his brother, then might he have been murdered by Morso by mistake? Had the real target been his big brother, Aldo? Equally importantly, as far as my new book was concerned, should I invent an Ernesto Morso lurking in the background of my ficti-tious murder victim?

After our drinks, I took Oscar back through the campsite to the beach, picking up a piece of driftwood on the way, and then spent ten minutes by the water's edge repeatedly throwing the stick into the sea for Oscar to swim out and retrieve. When even he was beginning to tire, we went back up the beach again and sat down alongside Anna. While I dug out Oscar's food bowl, she handed me a ham and cheese focaccia sandwich and passed on some interesting information.

'I've just been talking to Stefano, the advanced-class teacher – you know, the one with the dreadlocks. This is his summer job. He's been doing it now for four years while he finishes his university studies in Rome. He's another history fanatic like me, and he's doing archaeology. His special interest is the Etruscan period.'

I had heard of the Etruscans but knew very little about them. Anna must have seen the puzzled expression on my face and took pity on me.

'The Etruscan civilisation predates the Romans by five or six centuries. They occupied much of west and central Italy until the Romans finally assimilated them into their culture, granting them Roman citizenship. What Stefano was telling me was that for the Etruscans, Elba was very important indeed.'

I thought I'd better show that I was paying attention although, to be perfectly honest, I had just finished giving Oscar his lunch and was more interested in my sandwich. Two and a half hours falling off a sailboard certainly builds up an appetite. 'Was that because they were traders maybe? Presumably, Elba made a convenient stopping-off point.'

'I'm sure it did, but the importance of the island was its mines. Elba sits on top of some of the richest deposits of iron ore in the Mediterranean. Because of this, the island was of great importance not only to the Etruscans but also to the Greeks, the Romans, and subsequent rulers, all the way through the centuries. Anyway, what he told me was that there used to be a major Etruscan mining community just inland from here and he's been finding bits of Etruscan pottery on the beach and bigger pieces scattered across the seabed.' She looked up at me. 'You know you were telling me that those two uncommunicative guys at the hotel are *Carabinieri* from the TPC? Well, it occurred to me that this might be the reason why they're here. I wonder if somebody has been digging up Etruscan relics and selling them on the black market. Trading in antiquities is a criminal offence in Italy.'

This really was interesting – so interesting that I even put my sandwich down. 'I've been wondering what those two are doing here. That could well be it.' I glanced back over my shoulder towards the campsite. 'Aldo Graziani has spent an awful lot of money buying the land and investing in the infrastructure for his new all-singing all-dancing campsite, and I've been wondering where he got his money from. Do you think that Aldo might be a person of interest to the *Carabinieri* art squad?'

'Could be. There's a lot of money to be made in the illicit antiquities trade.' She caught my eye. 'Do you think his brother's death might somehow be connected with Etruscan objects?'

I was thinking along the same lines myself and I took my time before replying. Finally, I shook my head. 'It's an interesting theory but I can't really see how. Ignazio has been in prison for the last twenty years and he was only released last month. Now, if it had been *Aldo* who had ended up dead, there might well be a connection, but I can't see how Ignazio could have been involved with the sale of illegal artefacts. Of course, it might be that the murderer was actually aiming for Aldo, because of something to do with the antiquities trade, and killed the wrong man in the dark. If that were the case, I suppose that would indicate a link to the Etruscans. This afternoon, I'll talk it through with Virgilio and see what he thinks. It's certainly a coincidence, and I don't like coincidences in a murder inquiry.'

'And you still think it was murder?'

I didn't have to stop and think before answering. 'Yes, almost certainly, but it's still just an unproven hunch. As far as I can see, it most likely was committed by somebody connected with one of Ignazio's victims from twenty years ago who's been waiting patiently for the chance to get revenge. Don't forget, we're in a country where memories are long and grudges even longer. Alternatively, I'm tending to think that it might have been somebody closer to home. The fact is that his brother had clear motive for getting rid of him so as to inherit his share of the campsite and rid himself of a serious embarrassment. For Ignazio to conveniently fall off a cliff strikes me as distinctly suspicious.'

At that moment, Oscar jumped to his feet, tail wagging. I followed the direction of his nose and saw Virgilio and Lina approaching. They both made a fuss of Oscar, and Virgilio gave me a sympathetic smile.

'How did it go? Were you swimming with the fishes?' He grinned. 'I hear it's very popular with the criminal community.'

'I've done a lot of falling in, but less than yesterday.' I glanced across at Anna. 'To be honest, I even started enjoying myself a bit.' I turned back to Virgilio. 'What about you? Did you and Marco come up with anything new on our friend Graziani?'

'One or two interesting discoveries but nothing major. According to the prison log, during the whole of the twenty years that Graziani was behind bars, his brother never visited him even once. Clearly no love lost there, which makes it all the more peculiar – and suspicious – that the two brothers were dining together on Saturday night. Marco's still looking closely into each of Ignazio's four victims and any connections they might have had with the sort of people who go around pushing people off cliffs. So far nothing, but he's still looking. I spent half an hour with Rita checking the CCTV footage and there's no sign of anybody unexpected leaving the hotel and going in the direction of the clifftop. There's just you taking Oscar for his walk along with me and then me going out again and returning after eleven. Apart from us, there's just the victim of course, going out but not coming back, but none of the other guests or staff pop up on camera.'

I had been expecting as much. 'That means that if he was murdered by somebody at the hotel, they must have sneaked out through the trees so as to avoid the cameras. Checking the surveillance cameras implies a certain degree of professionalism, doesn't it? But how did the killer get out of the hotel in the first place? Presumably, the CCTV on the terrace doesn't show anybody going out that way and we know that the camera by the front door didn't either. Is there another way?'

Virgilio nodded. 'Rita and I discussed that. There are only two other doors: one from the kitchen that was firmly locked after the kitchen staff had gone home at ten, and a fire door, which is alarmed. I went for a little walkabout and discovered that there is a third possible exit, but it isn't a door. It's a big window on the first-floor landing leading out onto the roof of the outhouse behind. There's a stepladder conveniently propped up against the rear of the outhouse so our killer could have got out and back in again without being seen. I even climbed out through it myself to check that anybody could have done it.'

This at least proved that a determined guest or staff member at the

hotel could have been the murderer, and I added the obvious corollary.
'That means that if the killer was one of the guests, the murder was carefully planned and, once again, it shows professionalism or maybe inside
information. It might be worth doing a thorough investigation of all the
staff members who were around, including the owner. But there's another
possibility.' I went on to relate to him what I had heard this morning about
Ignazio pestering local women and maybe attempting to abduct a girl here
on the island twenty years ago, resulting in his being forced to leave for the
mainland. I also repeated what I'd heard in both bars about Aldo finding
the death of his brother most satisfactory, but that Aldo himself hadn't
been best liked either.

Virgilio listened with interest until I'd finished. 'This makes it even
more likely that Ignazio Graziani was *murdered* – whether mistaken for his
brother or on purpose remains to be seen. I need to pass all this information on to the inspector. I suppose it's possible that he already knows it, but
I have my doubts. The very least he should do is investigate the alleged
attempted abduction here on the island and find out if it really happened.
If so, is the girl – she must be a grown woman now – still around? Are her
family still here? Might they have been waiting twenty years to take the law
into their own hands?' I could hear the frustration in his voice, and I felt
the same way. If only we had been the investigating officers...

But, I told myself, we weren't. I was here on holiday and that was that.
This death was nothing to do with me.

11

MONDAY AFTERNOON

My afternoon windsurfing lesson wasn't as disastrous as I had expected, and by the end, I was definitely beginning to get the hang of tacking, although gybing defeated me. I still spent quite a lot of time in the water but I definitely began to feel that I was making progress. As for the Graziani case, I also felt that Virgilio and I were making progress, but there was a long way to go – starting with finding out whether the police had identified the murder weapon.

I got the answer to that question when Anna and I walked back to the hotel. I immediately saw that there were no longer any police vehicles in the car park and the expression on Virgilio's face when I spotted him on the terrace said it all.

'Half an hour ago, Inspector Bellini sent his sergeant to inform me that they've found no sign of a murder weapon and the pathologist is now agreeing with him that the wound to the back of the victim's head could have been caused in the fall. In consequence, as we thought, Bellini has effectively closed the case and put it down to misadventure – an unfortunate accident brought about principally by an excess of alcohol. By the sound of it, the pathologist reports that Graziani had consumed enough wine to sedate a rhino.'

I was secretly pleased and relieved that this went a long way towards removing the cloud that had been hanging over Virgilio's head and, although he wasn't showing it, I felt sure he must feel the same way.

While Anna went upstairs to take a shower, I sat down with Virgilio, with Oscar sprawled on the tiles at our feet. 'Did you have a chance to pass on to the inspector what we've discovered?'

'Not directly. I told the sergeant and he gave me the official line – "all avenues of investigation have been followed up and nothing suggests anything other than an accident". So Bellini has washed his hands of it.' He attracted the attention of the waiter and ordered two beers before adding a codicil. 'The sergeant let slip that Bellini is starting three weeks' leave tomorrow, taking a holiday in the USA and Canada with his wife and kids. That goes a long way towards explaining his readiness to draw a line under this case as soon as possible.' I could hear the frustration in his voice, and I felt the same way, but I did my best to conceal it.

'Well, you said it yourself, you're not sorry that Graziani's dead, so maybe the best thing to do is to just accept that and try to put the whole episode behind us.' This really didn't sound right to me at all, but I knew it was the sensible and pragmatic thing to do, even if it went totally against my principles.

Virgilio took his time replying, waiting until the waiter had brought our beers and a bowl of water for Oscar. He clinked his glass against mine, took a mouthful and looked me straight in the eye. 'It *was* murder, I just know it.'

I took a mouthful of beer and nodded. 'I agree. I'm convinced of it as well, but I can't prove it any more than you can.'

We sat in silence for a minute or two. I felt sure that both of us were thinking the same thing, but I chose to let him say it first. Finally, he made up his mind. 'Bellini is a fool and if I were his superior officer, I'd give him a kick up his lazy backside. I don't know about you, but, much as I would like to, I can't let it go. I need to know what happened.'

I reached over and clinked my glass against his, giving him a broad smile. 'I'm with you all the way so, *Commissario*, what's our next move?'

'The way I see it, I have a straightforward choice. I can contact the *Questore* in Livorno and see if I can get him to intervene, asking him to draft in an officer who's prepared to put in the legwork. The trouble is that, without any hard evidence, doing that could put the *Questore* in an awkward position. That sort of intervention would cause quite a lot of ill feeling – particularly as far as our friend Inspector Bellini's concerned – and I wouldn't want to make an enemy of anybody in the force if I can help it. I think you and I need to proceed on this on our own – if you're sure that Anna won't mind too much – and carry out our own investigation until we have something concrete. I have a perfectly valid warrant card that I can flash in order to arrange interviews with suspects, although it could get awkward if the word gets back to Bellini's people. Still, that's a risk I'm prepared to take.'

'Anna knows the score and she's happy for me to get involved. Apart from anything else, it's a matter of clearing your name.' We both knew full well that allegations, even unfounded and unproven allegations, can hang about and risk damaging a career. 'As a private investigator, I have every right to investigate whatever case I want, so why don't I do the sensitive stuff? The worst that can happen is for the police here to kick me off the island. The way I see it, the first person I'd like to interview is the victim's brother, Aldo. The more I think about it, the more I believe that he might have been involved. Maybe I could approach him saying that I've been engaged to look into Ignazio's death on behalf of somebody who prefers to remain anonymous. If I put it to him that I'm hoping he can provide me with some evidence that might help identify the killer, that should hopefully reassure him that we're not coming after him – at least not yet.'

Virgilio nodded in agreement. 'Sounds good to me. In the meantime, I'll call Marco and see if he's managed to find out anything more about our fellow guests. I would really like to sit down and talk to them one by one, but, now that the official line is that Graziani's death was an accident, that may not be so easy. And some of them may even be leaving in the morning. It would be good to get a feel for the people. You know how it is, Dan; you can tell a lot about someone simply from the look on their face.'

At that moment, the two *Carabinieri* officers appeared and sat down a couple of tables along from us. Virgilio and I exchanged glances, and he lowered his voice. 'Starting with these two. I think I'll go and ask them if they can spare me five minutes of their time. It's probably best if you don't accompany me as they may not want to talk about their mission in front of somebody they see as an outsider.'

'Definitely. While you're doing that, I'll go up and take a shower. After that, I want to see what I can find out about Aldo Graziani and his campsite.'

After a shower and a change, I opened the laptop and set about checking up on the victim's big brother. I started by accessing the campsite website and was impressed at its professionalism. Unless Aldo was a computer genius, he had probably paid somebody a lot of money to set this up. I was also impressed by the range of facilities. As well as the large pool and the bar/pizzeria, there were also two tennis courts, a business centre, boasting a high-speed Internet connection, a hair and beauty salon, and two smart, modern shower and toilet blocks, one including a sauna and hot tub. The place had certainly moved on a lot since the days of his father's little campsite for a couple of dozen tents.

Interestingly, I could find very little about Aldo himself. I couldn't even find a photo of him and it looked as though he was deliberately steering clear of social media. I didn't blame him for that, but it made my life more difficult. I found a few articles in the local newspaper and other online news outlets about the campsite but, again, virtually nothing about the owner. Although there were articles about Ignazio's death, most reported it either as an unfortunate accident or suicide. From what I'd heard today, everybody around here had known about his return to the island and where he'd been for the last twenty years and why, but most of the media had chosen to downplay his past and stick to Inspector Bellini's verdict of misadventure, no doubt much to the relief of his brother.

Anna had dozed off by this time, so Oscar and I quietly sneaked out of the room and went downstairs to Reception, where I was pleased to find Rita on her own.

'Rita, can I ask you something? I was talking to some men in the village earlier on and they told me that Ignazio Graziani was hounded off the island twenty years ago. He was making a nuisance of himself with a number of women and might even have attempted to abduct a girl here in Santa Sabina. Does that ring any bells with you?'

She looked shocked. 'Really? That's news to me. I was at university on the mainland at that time and I remember my parents telling me that Ignazio had been sent away, although they didn't go into any detail about why.' An expression of sadness spread across her face. 'I'm afraid my mother and father have both passed away now, so I can't ask them for any detail.'

'So you don't know if the attempted abduction story is true or not?'

'I'm sorry, I know nothing about that at all, but I can ask around if you like.'

I thanked her and brought up the other piece of information I'd gleaned today. 'I also heard that the victim's brother, Aldo, has a reputation as a womaniser. Does that sound familiar?'

An expression of distaste appeared on her face. 'A few years ago, definitely, but he's been keeping himself to himself more recently. He used to be a terror, quite amoral, and he treated some of the local girls and visiting tourists appallingly, taking advantage of them and then dumping them like rubbish. In fairness, he wasn't creepy like his brother; he just thought he was God's gift. It all came to a head when he took up with a married woman.'

Seeing that I wanted more, she continued. 'It was all very upsetting. It was just after his father's death when Aldo embarked on a relationship with a woman called Veronica Piccolo, but then her husband found out. There was the most awful bust-up and Veronica's husband punched Aldo so hard, it broke his nose. Aldo immediately dumped Veronica, and she was so desperate, she left her husband and two children and went off to the mainland. The last I heard of her, she was living and working in Venice. It must have been awful for her and, of course – those poor kids have grown up without a mother – and it's been very tough for her husband on his own, as you can imagine.' She sighed. 'What a mess – and all down to Aldo.'

'Was he married at that time?'

'Yes, he'd got married only a matter of a couple of years earlier. Poor woman.'

'Was that why their marriage came to an abrupt end?'

She nodded. 'His wife divorced him as soon as the affair blew up.' She shook her head sadly. 'Any woman would have done the same. Aldo's a louse, and he treated her appallingly.'

'Did she leave the island?'

'No, she's originally from Portoferraio and she went back there. I see her from time to time when I'm in town.'

I thanked her again and Oscar and I went out onto the terrace. There was no sign of Virgilio or the two *Carabinieri* officers, so I spent a bit of time checking a possible route from the window at the rear of the first-floor landing, over the top of the outhouse, around the back of the hotel and into the trees. From there, it was easy to see how somebody from the hotel could have made their way out to murder Ignazio Graziani, unseen by the cameras. Even so, I still couldn't rid myself of the feeling that the murderer might have been his own brother, and I did a bit of calculating. Virgilio had seen Ignazio alive at eleven o'clock, a full hour after the kitchen had closed and dinner had finished for everybody. What had the victim been doing, wandering about on the clifftop half an hour or more after the end of his meal? And where had his brother been?

I went back to Reception and had another word with Rita. 'Would I be right in thinking that you went off at ten on Saturday night?'

'Yes, along with the kitchen and serving staff. That's when the night porter comes on duty. Why do you ask?'

'I'm trying to work out where everybody was at the time of Graziani's death. Can you remember if there were many people out on the terrace when you went home?'

'Virtually nobody, as far as I can remember. Just a minute, let me pull up the CCTV footage for Saturday night. There's a camera on the terrace that should give us the answer.'

Sure enough, the only people left on the terrace after ten o'clock had been the amorous honeymoon couple, still lost in their own little world, and the table for three containing the victim, his brother and the young woman, Teresa. It was too dark to make out any great detail but I could see that Aldo was smoking a cigar, his brother nursing a glass of red wine and their female companion staring into the distance. I looked up at Rita. 'Can we find out at what time the Graziani brothers went inside, or did they go straight home?'

Obligingly, she spent five minutes checking the outside cameras until she finally managed to pick up Aldo and Teresa, heading back through the car park towards the main gate. We could only see them from behind, but his polo shirt and her long hair were unmistakable. The couple disappeared from sight at ten twenty-seven and the camera over the front door then showed the victim making his unsteady way along the path towards the clifftop and his death. I wondered why they had split up and so I asked Rita to go back through the footage of the terrace camera until we picked up the three of them at table again. As the time clock showed ten-fourteen, a furious argument appeared to erupt and both men were soon waving their arms about in considerable animation. At exactly ten twenty-five, Aldo and Teresa stood up and left Ignazio at the table, still waving his arms about. He finally subsided into silence, emptied the last of the bottle of wine into his glass and drank deeply. It was ten forty-six when he rose unsteadily to his feet and headed around to the front door and onto the path towards the cliffs.

A thought occurred to me. 'You said that Aldo often comes here for dinner. Does he normally walk in and out through the main gates, or is there a shortcut?'

'When he's with Teresa, he usually uses the main gate through the car park and that's covered by the camera. Apart from that, there's only the pedestrian gate at the clifftop.'

'But that's limited to hotel guests and it needs a code to open it, doesn't it? Do you think Aldo knows the code?'

'I'm sure he does. It's been the same for years, and I've seen him coming and going that way. To be honest, a lot of locals know the code as well. Signor Silvano doesn't mind.'

It was potentially very interesting that the code appeared to be common knowledge around here, so the locked gate wasn't in fact as much of a hurdle as we'd thought. Given that Aldo had left the hotel at ten twenty-seven, it was no more than a ten-minute walk to the campsite. He would have had time to leave Teresa at her accommodation, wherever that was, and make his way back to the clifftop through the trees, using the pedestrian gate and the not-so-secret code. Unless Teresa could come up with a convincing alibi for him, this meant that Aldo Graziani had, not only a convincing motive, but also the opportunity to kill his brother. Maybe *he* had been the figure lurking in the shadows when Virgilio had punched Ignazio. As for means, Ignazio had been so drunk, it would have been relatively easy for anyone to push him over the edge. As far as I was concerned, motive, means and opportunity added up to a pretty damning indictment of Aldo.

'What about Teresa? Does she live in the villa with Aldo?'

'Not officially, but who knows? As I understand it, she lives in one of the chalets, but whether she sleeps there or at the villa is another matter.'

So it would have been easy for Aldo to see Teresa back to her chalet and then slip off again and murder his brother. Another thought struck me. 'Where did the other people go when they left the terrace? Did they go to the bar, did they go out, or did they go to their rooms?'

This time, Rita switched to Saturday night's CCTV camera in Reception, and we could see that from nine-thirty onwards, a steady stream of people had left the terrace, walked through the dining room, crossed the hall, and climbed the stairs or taken the lift to the first and second floors. I counted them on my fingers and there could be no doubt about it: apart from the pair of lovers and the Graziani brothers still outside on the terrace, everybody else had disappeared upstairs to their rooms by ten at the very latest. I double-checked with Rita, but she confirmed my fear that there was no CCTV on the upper floors, so there was no record of anybody moving about and maybe climbing out of the big window on the first-floor landing. So, potentially, almost any of the guests could have sneaked out unseen but, even so, the idea that we could be looking at a case of fratricide wouldn't go away.

* * *

Virgilio and I met up before dinner and I passed on what I had discovered before asking him how it had gone with the two *Carabinieri* officers. His answer was fascinating.

'As we thought, they're here on a mission, and Anna was right about the Etruscans. The TPC have been investigating the appearance on the world antiques market of a number of high-value Etruscan pieces – statues mostly, but also beautifully decorated plates and vases. They haven't been flooding the market but have been turning up every now and then for the past four or five years. Their investigations have led the *Carabinieri* to believe that the origin of these objects is here on the island.'

'So why come to Santa Sabina in particular?'

'They had to get the all-clear from their superiors before they could tell me. That took a while but it finally came through. It appears that they've been following the money all the way back from a dealer in Lugano, Switzerland, to a known trafficker in Bologna. They've arrested the trafficker, and the man has been singing like a canary. Apparently, he's been buying from a handler in Tuscany who in turn has a contact on the island of Elba who supplies him with the goods. Although no names have been mentioned, the finger of suspicion has been pointing at this part of the island.'

This of course tied in even more precisely with what Anna's windsurfing teacher had been saying about there possibly having been an Etruscan settlement close by.

'Do they suspect Aldo Graziani?'

'Not specifically, but they think it must have been somebody in this area, and Graziani's one of the biggest landowners. Of course, just because it's his land, doesn't necessarily mean that he's been doing the digging. Have you ever heard of *tombaroli*?' I shook my head, and he explained. 'Literally tomb robbers, they're normally the bottom step of the pyramid. They dig up the artefacts and sell them to a local handler who in turn sells them on to a bigger trafficker, and so it continues all the way up to the top.'

'And the top is...?'

'Private collectors and bona fide museums. By faking provenance – swearing that the objects have been in the possession of individuals or families for decades – the artefacts can be sold to respectable institutions around the world. Apparently, everybody in the trade knows that it happens, and in spite of some recent legislation in some overseas countries, most notably the US, it still continues to this day.'

'And presumably it's a lucrative trade?'

'As an example, the *Carabinieri* told me that a good Etruscan statue was sold only last year for seven million dollars. It's certainly lucrative – especially if you're up near the top of the pyramid.'

'Wow, I had no idea they could be worth so much. And did the Bologna trafficker give them the name of the handler in Tuscany?'

There was scepticism written across Virgilio's face as he shook his head. 'He claims not to know it. He says everything was done online with fake names, and payment was made to a numbered account in the Cayman Islands. This sounds highly unlikely, so the *Carabinieri* are still pressurising him to come up with a name, but so far, no joy.'

This was fascinating. 'The more I think about it, the more convinced I am that this trade could be the way that Aldo Graziani has managed to pay for the expansion of his holiday resort.'

The potential evidence against Aldo Graziani was mounting up, and I knew that I would pay him a visit early next morning. First of all, I had to decide how I would describe myself to him. If I told him I was a PI, he might clam up. Was there some way I could get him to speak to me without revealing my true identity? This also got me thinking about my book and I wondered if I could somehow bring the illegal antiques trade into it. One way or another, it could be that Ignazio Graziani was doing me a favour.

12

TUESDAY MORNING

Next morning dawned bright and sunny once again, but there was quite a bit more wind. As Oscar and I walked along the clifftop to the windsurfing beach, I could see waves breaking against the rocky headland and a fishing boat yawing from side to side. This didn't bode well for today's windsurfing session. Even worse, from what I could see, the wind had changed direction, and it looked as though there was every possibility that I could be washed out to sea when I inevitably fell off. Although I had been looking forward to today's session, I had no desire to end up on a one-way ticket to the other side of the Mediterranean – or the bottom of it.

Before going down to the beach to give Oscar an early-morning swim, I walked up into the campsite, where people were just beginning to stir. What interested me was the building behind the bar. A wooden sign in the shape of a pointing finger indicated that this housed Reception. Hopefully, this would be where I would be able to find Aldo Graziani. It was a quarter past seven, but the glass door was locked, even though a sign on it indicated that it should have opened at seven. I was still standing there considering what to do next when a female voice made me turn.

'Isn't it open yet? That's a bit strange.' Although I had never seen her close up, I immediately sensed that the trim little woman with the long hair standing in front of me was Teresa, Aldo's dinner companion, employee and possibly more than that. I shook my head ruefully.

'I was hoping I could have a word with Signor Graziani, but I seem to have come a bit too early.'

She gave me an apologetic shrug and pulled out a bunch of keys with which she unlocked the door. I followed her inside where she returned her attention to me. 'Signor Graziani's normally here by now. I wonder what's keeping him. Can I help? My name's Teresa; I'm his PA.'

Seeing her close up in the light of day, I realised she was probably a bit older than I had thought, maybe in her mid- or late thirties. She was an attractive woman with a glossy mane of black hair cascading down well below her shoulders. She was being polite, but there was a hard glint in her eyes. Somehow, I got the feeling she wouldn't be easy to push around.

I had been debating what story to use but without a great deal of success, so in the end, I opted for the truth – or at least a version of it. 'My name is Armstrong, I'm a private investigator from Florence and I'd like to speak to Signor Graziani on a personal matter.'

A wary look instantly appeared on her face. 'What sort of personal matter?'

'I'm sorry, but I'm not at liberty to mention that.'

'It's about Ignazio, his brother, isn't it?' The expression on her face changed to one of regret, but somehow, I had a feeling that she wasn't really sorry about what had happened to her boss's brother. I did my best to sound clueless.

'Why should it be about him? After all, he's dead, isn't he?'

She gave a little hiss of frustration and leant back against the counter. 'And I'm glad he's dead.' She looked up and caught my eye. 'Really, I am. He was a horrible man.'

'But he was your boss's brother, wasn't he? Surely he can't have been that bad.' I already knew the answer to this, but I was keen to see what kind of response I could provoke from her.

'You know he'd just come out of prison, don't you?' She saw me nod and she continued. 'Then I'm sure you know the awful things he did to those poor girls. Every time I saw him, I had a mental image of what I'd read in the papers back when I was a teenager. He was a monster and, I'll tell you this, death was the best thing that could have happened to him before he did something like that again – and he would have done, I just know it. The way he looked at me was terrifying.' She shook her head, presumably in an attempt to remove bitter memories of Ignazio Graziani, and took a deep breath. 'Anyway, like I say, he's gone and I'm glad, but that's why you want to speak to Aldo, isn't it?'

'I'm afraid I can't go into specifics, but it would be good to speak to him. Would it be possible to make an appointment to see him? I can come back any time.'

The wary look was back on her face again and when she spoke, she sounded doubtful. 'I'm afraid I can't make an appointment until I've spoken to him. He's a very private person, you see.'

I did my best to produce a friendly smile. 'So am I. Why don't I come back again in an hour or so and see if he's around?'

She still looked far from convinced but, reluctantly, she nodded. 'You could try, but, like I say, he does tend to keep himself to himself.'

I thanked her and headed back down to the beach with Oscar, reflecting on the encounter with Teresa. It was clear that she had despised and disliked her boss's brother intensely, and I found myself wondering whether this antipathy might have been sufficient for her to consider murder, although this seemed hardly credible considering that Ignazio had returned to the island only a month ago. There had, however, been that hard glint in her eye that made me think that she might indeed have been the type to take such drastic action. But why? Had Ignazio maybe tried it on with her? Anything was possible.

Oscar and I walked along the water's edge and, as usual, I picked up bits of driftwood and threw them for him to swim out and retrieve. Remembering what Anna had told me about the Etruscans, I kept my eyes open for pieces of ancient pottery but found nothing of interest until we reached the very end of the beach, well beyond the last of the parasols and sunbeds. Here, the sand gave way to another rocky outcrop and the waves were splashing against the rocks. I was just about to turn around and head back to the hotel for some breakfast when my eye was drawn to something out in the white water. At first sight, it looked as though somebody had lost a surfboard but as the waves pushed it closer to the shore, I suddenly realised that this was no surfboard.

This was a body, floating face down in the water.

Pulling off my shoes and tucking my phone, keys and wallet inside them, I ran into the water and swam out through the waves accompanied by a joyful Oscar, who was obviously pleased to have company. The waves weren't enormous but they were very confused and the swell risked smashing me into the rocks. By the time I reached the body, I felt as if I had been in a tumble dryer. I caught hold of a hand and started pulling. It was hard going, but I finally managed to get back close enough to the shore to be able to touch the seabed with my feet and walk the last few yards. I took hold of the other hand and dragged the body clear of the waves before subsiding on the sand for a breather. It had been hard work.

My moment of relaxation didn't last long as Oscar came up to within a couple of feet of me and shook himself vigorously. The cold shower roused me and I got to my feet. I went over to kneel down alongside the body so as to take a closer look at it. It was a man with dark hair and there was a nasty bruise and a vicious wound to the back of his head. I gently rolled the head towards me and felt a shiver go through me as I was confronted by something quite unexpected. It was with a spooky feeling of déjà vu that I realised that the man I was looking at was Ignazio Graziani, rapist and jailbird.

No sooner had I made this discovery than I reminded myself that this was impossible. Only two mornings ago, I had seen Ignazio's body lying on the rocks by the hotel beach, after which the pathologist had taken it to the morgue, so there were only two other logical explanations. Either I was going doolally, or this had to be Ignazio's brother, Aldo. Although Anna might have views to the contrary, I decided on balance that the latter was more likely to be the case.

I sat back on my heels and took stock. This was the first time I'd seen Aldo Graziani's face clearly, and the resemblance between the two brothers was uncanny. I knew that they hadn't been twins but, even though there had been a couple of years between them, Aldo was a dead ringer for Ignazio. He was still wearing a polo shirt but, apart from his appearance, the other thing that struck me was the manner of his death, so similar to his brother's. It was the same old conundrum – had it been an accident, suicide, or murder? The wound to the back of the head made suicide unlikely – it isn't easy to hit yourself like that. An accident was a possibility if he had fallen and cracked his skull, but I had a strong suspicion that somebody had done that for him. My money was on this being a second murder. I reached for my shoes, pulled out my phone and called Virgilio. He answered almost immediately.

'*Ciao*, Dan, what's new?'

'*Ciao*, Virgilio, there's been another death and this time, it's the brother.'

'Aldo Graziani dead?' He sounded surprised, but maybe not that surprised. 'How did it happen?'

I told him where I was and how I'd had to swim out to recover the body. As I was speaking, it occurred to me that if I hadn't spied the body and it had managed to get around the headland, there would probably have been nothing but open sea between it and Sicily or even North Africa. It might never have been found.

Virgilio listened in silence until I had finished and then he spoke.

'Can you stay with the body? I'll call the police now and I'll meet you there in fifteen minutes.'

In fact, Virgilio got to me in little more than ten minutes. He must have run all the way. Oscar trotted off to greet him when he spotted him coming along the beach, and I was touched to see that Virgilio had even thought to bring me a towel. As I did my best to dry myself off, he checked the body and came to the same conclusion that I had.

'The two brothers are like two peas in a pod. Are you thinking what I'm thinking?'

I nodded. 'How about this scenario? On Saturday night, somebody set out to murder, not Ignazio, but *Aldo* Graziani. In the dark on the clifftop, the killer mistook one for the other and killed the wrong man. Realising his mistake, the murderer came here last night or early this morning and made up for it. What do you think?'

'I think you could well be right. One thing's for sure: I can't believe that both brothers decided to end it all, or that they both had accidents in almost the same place, on almost the same day. I'm convinced that we're looking at two murders and, as you say, it's quite possible that both were committed by the same perpetrator.'

'The question is – why?'

'Why indeed?'

I began to hear sirens in the distance. 'It'll be interesting to see who takes charge of the case now that Inspector Bellini has gone off to Canada. Hopefully, somebody with a bit more imagination.'

Virgilio grunted. 'And a bit more enthusiasm.'

13

TUESDAY MORNING

The police arrived in two blue and white squad cars. They stopped at the entrance to the beach, and I saw two people get out of the first one and start running towards us while the two occupants of the second car followed at a more sedate pace.

The first person to reach us was the same uniformed sergeant we had already met, and Virgilio gave him a grim smile.

'Good morning, Sergeant Gallo. We meet again.'

'You seem to collect corpses, *Commissario*.' Gallo shook hands with both of us before looking down at the body. 'Well, well, so you say you think this is Aldo Graziani. Now, there's a coincidence.' From his sceptical tone, it was clear that he felt the same way that we did.

Virgilio nodded in agreement. 'I've never liked coincidences, Gallo. Are you the investigating officer now?'

The sergeant shook his head and pointed back along the beach. 'No, that's Inspector Fontana.' From his tone, it sounded to me as if he wasn't too sure about Bellini's replacement, and my spirits sank. Bellini had been bad enough, but if the new inspector was even worse, the chances of a rapid conclusion to the investigation seemed unlikely. However, rather than put him on the spot, I took a closer look at the two figures coming along the beach towards us: a young constable in uniform and an older man in plain clothes, walking with a limp.

'Is that him there?' Gallo nodded and I gave him a prompt. 'Have you worked alongside him for long?'

He glanced at his watch and gave me a hint of a smile in reply. 'About twenty-five minutes. He arrived from Livorno last night and this is his first day. He's what you might call a stopgap while Inspector Bellini is away.'

As the two men approached, I could see that Inspector Fontana looked some years older than me, probably well into his sixties. He had a fine head of steel-grey hair and he was walking with the aid of a stick. When he reached us, Sergeant Gallo started to make the introductions, but Inspector Fontana cut him off.

'Thank you, Gallo, but the *commissario* and I already know each other.' He held out his hand towards Virgilio and gave him a broad smile. '*Ciao*, Virgilio, it's very good to see you again, and congratulations on your promotion.'

To my surprise, Virgilio reached out with both arms and gave the inspector a bearhug. '*Ciao*, Piero, long time no see. How're you doing?'

'I'm okay, thanks.' There was a note of something in the inspector's voice that could have been regret, but before I could dwell on it, he turned towards me and held out his hand. 'And are you the gentleman who found the body?'

Virgilio was quick to specify. 'He's actually the man who leapt into the sea fully clothed and swam out to grab the body before it was washed away. He's a good friend of mine: Dan Armstrong, from Florence.'

Fontana and I shook hands, and he raised an eyebrow in my direction. 'Armstrong isn't a common Florentine name.' There was a twinkle in his eyes, and I smiled back.

'I'm British and I moved to Tuscany three years ago.'

'And that's how you know Virgilio?'

'That's right. We have a lot in common.'

'I'm pleased to meet you, and my thanks to you for swimming out to retrieve the victim.' His attention switched back to Virgilio and he pointed at the body. 'I gather you believe this to be Aldo Graziani. Did you know him well?'

'This is the first time I've seen him close up, but the resemblance to his brother is unmistakable.' Virgilio went on to produce a quick summary of the events of the last few days, and I was pleased to hear that the inspector had already started familiarising himself with the case. Fontana listened impassively until Virgilio finished, and then he asked the million-dollar question. 'So, do you think this death is suspicious?'

We both nodded in unison and Virgilio replied. 'Dan and I are both convinced that this death and the death of the man's brother three nights ago were murder.'

'You believe Ignazio Graziani was murdered even though his death has currently been dismissed as an unfortunate accident?'

Virgilio nodded. 'Indeed, but, in light of this latest death, my feeling is that the original decision needs to be reevaluated. Two deaths in short succession – both members of the same family and both so similar in execution – strike me as decidedly suspicious.' He stopped. 'But it's your investigation, Piero; it's up to you. I don't want to get under your feet, but if I can give any help, just say the word.'

'Thank you, Virgilio, but aren't you on holiday?'

'Yes, but the offer still stands. Dan has a windsurfing lesson this morning, but I'd be happy to stick around and talk you through what we've found out over the past two days. We think it could well be that the same perpetrator has been responsible for both deaths.'

I left the two of them together and set off back to the hotel with Oscar, where I found Anna out on the terrace, sipping a cappuccino. I saw her eyes register the fact that my clothes were dripping wet, and she shot me an ironic smile. 'Been swimming, Dan? Remind me to tell you about swimming trunks. They're a lot more convenient than diving into the sea fully clothed.'

I told her what had happened and she rolled her eyes. 'So one dead body wasn't enough for you. You had to go and find yourself another one.'

I shook my head ruefully. 'I'm sorry, *carissima*, but you know how it is.'

Now it was her turn to look rueful. 'Oh yes, I know exactly how it is. You have the same nose for murder as Oscar does for food.'

Hearing his name and the word 'food' in the same sentence sent Oscar across to position himself primly alongside her where he gave her his *I'm starving* look. As usual, it worked, and Anna handed him down a biscuit before looking up at me. 'It's probably a good idea if you go and get changed. I'll look after Oscar.'

I did as I was told and all the time that I was in our room, I kept turning over in my head how this most recent development affected our investigation – and I really did think of it as *our* investigation now. Although the scenario I had painted for Virgilio of a single killer being responsible for both murders seemed most probable, I did my best to consider the alternatives. If the murders were unconnected – and that seemed improbable under the circumstances – the most likely motive for murdering the first victim was probably some form of revenge for what he'd done twenty years earlier. Of course, it was still possible that Ignazio had been murdered by his brother, who had then taken his own life in a fit of remorse – although striking yourself on the back of the head is far from straightforward. Alternatively, maybe Aldo had killed his brother, and then somebody else had killed *him*.

But why? Assuming that Aldo had killed his brother, was it possible that somebody had decided to avenge that death? So far, I hadn't come across anybody with a good word to say about Ignazio Graziani, but that didn't mean that there wasn't one lurking somewhere. Could Ignazio have had some sort of love interest here on the island? Considering that he'd been in prison for twenty years and had been released only a few weeks ago, it was either somebody so deeply in love with him that she had waited for him all this time, or it had been a whirlwind romance that had developed over the past couple of weeks. Either way, I was sceptical.

Then there was the Etruscan antiquities question. Could there be a connection between either or both deaths and the investigation being carried out by the *Carabinieri*? For a moment, I even found myself questioning whether maybe the two plain-clothes officers might have taken the law into their own hands but, again, this seemed highly unlikely – but not impossible. And, of course, Aldo had somehow managed to make himself a lot of money, and wealth can bring envy and bitterness. What about this Ernesto Morso, who had allegedly been forced into selling his land? Had he taken his revenge? But why wait five years to do so? Maybe Aldo Graziani had been killed by a disgruntled staff member or a relative of one of the women he had allegedly treated so poorly – even his ex-wife?

By the time I had showered and changed into dry clothes, my head was spinning with suspects.

When I got back to the terrace, I found that Lina had joined Anna, so I helped myself to a plate of scrambled eggs and bacon and sat down with them. The aroma of bacon instantly brought Oscar to my side, doing his best to look underfed and unloved. As I handed him down a piece of bacon rind – he and I have an agreement that rinds belong to him – I discovered that the two women had been discussing this latest twist in the Graziani case.

Lina was the first to comment. 'I'll be quite honest, Dan: up till now, I've tended to believe that the first murder was nothing more than a drunken accident, just as the police said, but this second death has changed my mind. It's too much of a coincidence.'

Anna had been thinking along the same lines as me. 'You said that the two brothers looked very similar, didn't you, Dan? Could it be that the first murder was a mistake? The killer got the wrong man and so he went back and did it properly the second time?'

I nodded. 'That's what I'm tending to think as well, but there's the question of why. There's an obvious motive for killing Ignazio in revenge for what he did to those women twenty years ago, but what possible motive could there have been for somebody to want to kill his brother?'

While I had my breakfast, we discussed the two cases and the similarities between them, but we were unable to make any kind of breakthrough.

I was just finishing a bowl of excellent fresh fruit salad when Virgilio reappeared. After helping himself to some food, he sat down with us.

'I've spent half an hour talking Piero Fontana through everything we've discovered, and it sounds as though he's in agreement with us that both deaths were suspicious. He's given orders that all guests should stay at the hotel, and his people are now questioning everybody at the campsite and on the beach to find out if anybody saw anything, heard anything or can come up with any idea why Aldo Graziani might have been targeted. The pathologist has already removed the body, and she's promised to do the post-mortem straight away. Hopefully, this will supply us with information about when and how he died – was it straightforward accidental drowning or something more? And you and I know what we think.'

This sounded good to me. 'At least Inspector Fontana is taking it seriously – unlike his predecessor. It's convenient that you two know each other. Was that from your days in Pisa?'

Virgilio nodded. 'I worked alongside him there when I first started in the force. He's a good man and a hard worker. I'm sure he'll do a good job here.' A more serious expression appeared on his face. 'If it hadn't been for the accident, I have little doubt he would have been a *commissario* himself now.'

'What accident? What happened to him?' Anna asked the question that was on my lips.

'A road traffic accident, a bad one. It was a high-speed chase that went wrong. He was driving, but it was no fault of his. One of the front tyres of the squad car blew out and the car spun off the road into a tree at full speed. The officer alongside him was killed outright and Piero was badly injured – spinal problems – and spent months in hospital. As a result, when he was finally allowed to return to service, it was clear that he'd never fully recover from his mobility issues, so they shifted him down to Livorno and stuck him in Admin. I'm sure he's been good at what he's been doing for the last twenty years, but the accident cut short a very promising career. He's been telling me how happy he is to get back to the sharp end at long last – even if it's just for a few weeks. The main thing is that we can be quite sure he'll put in the effort that Bellini didn't.'

14

TUESDAY

My windsurfing career took a turn for the better that day. It was as if my brain had finally accepted the logic of what I was supposed to be doing, and I found myself able not only to go up and down the beach in a straight line but also to turn around and come back again. I'm sure it wasn't pretty, but by the time our lunch break came along, I was feeling positively ebullient – and a lot less full of salt water than previous days. More to the point, Anna had obviously been watching and she gave me her seal of approval.

'I told you we'd make a windsurfer out of you, didn't I, Dan? You looked really good out there.'

I was under few illusions as to how good I might have looked, but I thanked her all the same and decided that this merited a real beer rather than a low-alcohol one for a change. At that moment, Ingrid came walking past with Anna's teacher, Stefano, and I asked them if they would like to join us. After ordering the drinks, I sat back and listened as the subject inevitably turned to the sudden death of their boss, the owner of the windsurfing school, campsite and villa. I was interested to see that, although both looked shocked, neither looked particularly saddened by the event, and Ingrid didn't even bother trying.

'I'll be quite honest, Dan: if that had been you or your lovely Labrador lying dead on the beach, I would have been a lot more surprised and a lot more upset.'

Oscar had positioned himself alongside her with his nose on her knee, staring up at her in adoration. Doing my best not to sound like a private detective, I prompted her into elaborating.

'Wasn't he a very nice man? I never met him.'

She screwed up her face. 'I know we shouldn't speak ill of the dead but, no, he wasn't a very nice man.' I saw her glance across at Stefano for a moment. 'At least not if you were a woman.'

'So he was a bit of a Casanova, was he?'

'A *bit*?' She shuddered. 'Ask any of the women who work here. The one thing we all learnt from day one was never to find yourself alone with him. He was like an octopus – hands all over the place.'

'Oh dear.' I was still trying to sound less like a detective and more like a shocked bystander. 'And did he try it on with you?'

This time, Stefano answered. 'He tried it on with every woman in the place. It was disgusting, but jobs like this are hard to find so, like Ingrid says, the girls just learned to avoid him where possible.'

'And did they all avoid him, or did anybody go along with his advances? After all, I imagine he was quite a wealthy man.'

Again, the two of them exchanged glances before Ingrid replied. 'You would probably do well to put that question to Teresa, his PA.'

I didn't want to press them any further so I took a sip of beer and let Anna turn the conversation to the Etruscans. I listened with interest as she and Stefano discussed the Etruscan mining community who had quite possibly lived near here two thousand years ago and from time to time, I asked a question or two.

'When you say, "near here", where exactly do you mean? Are there ruins we could visit? I'm sure Anna would enjoy that, wouldn't you?'

She nodded and Stefano pointed inland. 'On the other side of the main road, just past Graziani's villa, there are clear traces of early mining. Where there are mines, there are normally smelting furnaces, and it would be amazing if I could find the remains of one of these, what the locals call *fabbrichili*. There might even have been the site of a settlement there, but I haven't seen any traces so far.'

'And what about the mines; what are they like?'

'The whole mountain behind us is riddled with them. Most are not much more than depressions in the ground these days. Most of the deeper ones have long since collapsed, but you can still make out some of the slag heaps. Nowadays, they're overgrown, but if you look at the hillside carefully, you'll soon see little mounds and dips everywhere.'

'What about the miners themselves? You mentioned a settlement. Do you think that might be up there as well?'

He smiled. 'That's what I'd love to find out. I'm writing my thesis on the Etruscan communities here on the island and I would dearly like to be able to pinpoint a former settlement. Who knows? They might have lived only a matter of metres from where we are now.' He sounded wistful and I was impressed at his dedication to his subject.

I sat back and listened with one ear while considering what he'd said. If there had been mines and a smelting furnace close to where Graziani's new villa now stood, could it be that he had discovered the remains of the settlement, dug up valuable artefacts, and lived off the proceeds? I resolved to take Oscar for a walk up there this afternoon after finishing my next windsurfing lesson.

* * *

By the time my afternoon session finished – and I had been delighted to find that I had been able to cope with the stronger wind and the choppier conditions – I was feeling ever more positive about my progress – at least as far as windsurfing was concerned. When it came to the two murders, I was less optimistic. There were still too many unanswered questions and I wondered how Virgilio and his former colleague were getting on. Hopefully, Inspector Fontana's investigation would unearth new information.

After a long, cool, glass of sparkling mineral water, I left Anna, who told me she was feeling tired and wanted to head back to the hotel. Oscar and I walked up through the campsite until we reached the main road. When I say main road, I don't mean that it was a busy highway by any means, and Oscar and I were able to cross without seeing a single vehicle. The vegetation on the other side of the road was in stark contrast to the neatly mown grass and well-maintained flower beds of the campsite, and I found myself walking up a vestigial track through what had once been a vineyard. Now, after years of neglect, the vines had run wild and spread out across the ground, some encroaching onto the track. Apart from ruts made by a 4 x 4 or an agricultural vehicle of some kind heading up to an agricultural shed, the track looked as though it was very little used, and I could imagine that in a year or two, it might even disappear underneath the rampant vines.

It was very hot up here away from the sea breeze and Oscar appeared happy to trot alongside me rather than go bounding off into the undergrowth. I was pleased about this because I had read that there were several species of poisonous snakes here in the hills, and the last thing I wanted was for him to get bitten. I'm not a fan of snakes, poisonous or not, but fortunately, the only reptiles we came across were terrified lizards who shot off as our shadows landed on them. The laws of physics told me that my black dog would soon find the direct sunlight uncomfortable, so I just walked up to the top of a slight incline from where I had a better view onwards up the hillside. Here there was a wonderful gnarled old pine tree whose trunk was about the same thickness as my waist and was probably twice as old as I was – maybe more. We stopped in the welcome shade and I took a look around.

With my back to the sea, hiding Graziani's villa and the campsite from view, there was virtually no sign of human activity apart from the large shed, which had probably once been used by the farmer. Seen relatively close up, it was more modern than I had thought, and I studied it critically. I had been thinking about getting a shed of my own, although I would need something only a fraction of the size of this serious agricultural building, and this sort of simple, practical design looked ideal. I took a couple of photos and resolved to show them to Nello, the local carpenter back in my village, in the hope that he could make me something similar. As I did so, I wondered idly why anybody had bothered to stick a solid-looking shed like this in the middle of an abandoned field – and the field was definitely abandoned.

The field was covered with a mixture of old vines, weeds, heather and thorny bushes that would have made any attempt at walking off the track almost impossible. The earth beneath my feet was a dusty orange colour and the stones littering the slope were a faded deep red – no doubt a sign of the ore beneath. Ahead of me, the hillside rose more sharply and carried on right up to the distant summit of what my phone told me was Monte Calamita, which translates as the magnetic mountain. It was the richness of the minerals beneath my feet that had made Elba one of the most important places in early Mediterranean civilisation, and I could almost feel the history radiating up through my feet as I trod in the footsteps of the long-lost miners.

Remembering what Stefano had said, I squinted hard and gradually started to make out occasional mounds marking old slag heaps and mines. Some were barely a few feet high, one or two almost as big as the shed. I let my eyes range about, but I was unable to spot any sign of a smelting furnace – although I didn't really know what I was looking for. My eyes were drawn to a darker patch of earth where the vegetation was even thicker than elsewhere. On closer inspection, it was clear that this was a spring as I could see water oozing out through the ground and trickling off downhill towards the sea. The land itself was slightly flatter here and it occurred to me that the combination of level ground and fresh water might well have made this an ideal place for an Etruscan mining community. I could imagine a cluster of primitive homes up here but, alas, without stripping all the greenery away, it was impossible to identify any traces of human habitation so, after a fruitless search, I headed back downhill again, determined to mention the spring to Stefano in the hope that it might help his research.

As Oscar and I walked down through the campsite, I made a little detour and visited the reception building once more. I was interested to see how Teresa the PA had taken the death of her boss. If it was true that she had had a romantic involvement with him, I was expecting to find her in tears. Instead, I found her behind the counter doing something on the computer while, bizarrely, 1980s band Black Lace belted out 'Agadoo' from a speaker behind her. She looked up as I came in and gave me a beaming smile. For a moment, I even wondered if she might still be unaware of Aldo's death, because I certainly hadn't been expecting to see her looking so cheerful.

Or had I? After all, I only had it on hearsay that she might have had an involvement with victim number two. Maybe her feelings towards her boss had been similar to those of Ingrid at the windsurfing school. Could it be that she was now relieved that her sex-pest boss was no longer around?

I walked over to the counter and was pleased to see her reach out and turn down the volume of the music. As it was, I had a feeling I was going to be humming the annoyingly addictive – if incomprehensible – lyrics for the next few days.

'Hello again. How was your windsurfing?'

'Good, thanks.' I hadn't told her that I was doing a windsurfing course, so presumably. this meant that she had been checking up on me. If so, why? Dismissing this for now, I returned to the matter in hand. 'I was sorry to hear the news of Signor Graziani's death. It sounds like it was another unfortunate accident.'

The cheerful smile left her face. 'Who knows?'

I had a feeling that she knew more than she was saying and I did my best to find out what that might be. 'Now that he's dead, I'm unable to ask him the questions I wanted, and I wondered if you would mind answering them for me – if you can, of course?'

'What sort of questions?' That hard look was back in her eyes again. 'I only worked with him. If it was anything of a personal nature, he would never have confided in me.' She must have spotted scepticism on my face. 'I imagine you've been talking to people who say that Aldo and I were an item. Well, I can categorically tell you what I told the police earlier today: we weren't. Yes, I spent quite a lot of time with him, but only as far as my job demanded.'

I remained not totally convinced but left it at that for now. 'My questions are mostly about his brother. Could you tell me how relations were between Aldo and Ignazio? I've been staying at the Augustus and I'm pretty sure I saw you there the other night having dinner with both brothers. Did that mean that they were close?'

She shook her head. 'Anything but – Ignazio's return to the island was the last thing Aldo wanted. Take a look around. This is a good business, and he's built it up almost from scratch. The arrival of his brother fresh out of jail came as a most unwelcome shock.'

'But Aldo gave him a bed and even took him out for dinner. Surely that means there was still a degree of brotherly love there?'

'I've already told this to the police. Last Saturday night was supposed to be their farewell dinner. I don't know the details but, as I understand it, Aldo promised his brother money on condition that he left the island and never came back.' She bent down and opened a drawer, sifted through a few papers, before producing a ticket. 'Look, here's the ferry ticket that Aldo asked me to book for Ignazio.' She pointed to it. 'See the date? Sunday morning.'

It occurred to me that this carefully preserved ticket was a convenient piece of evidence in support of Aldo's alibi – if he had indeed killed his brother. Little details like this go down well in a court of law. Of course, there was no proof that Teresa had bought the ticket on Aldo's orders. What if she had arranged the alibi for herself, and I was talking to Ignazio's murderer – and maybe a double murderer at that? Small and dainty she might be, but she couldn't hide that hard expression in her eyes.

I chose my words carefully when I asked the next question. 'Can I take it that when you and Aldo left the Augustus on Saturday night, you both returned here?'

She shook her head. 'We both came back in this direction, but I went to my chalet while he returned to his villa.' She looked up and caught my eye for a moment. 'And, before you ask, no, I didn't join him in his villa. I hope I've made myself clear as far as my relationship with him was concerned.'

If she was telling the truth, this opened the door to Aldo easily having had time to sneak back and murder his brother on Saturday night. But who then murdered *him* two days later? And, of course, there was always the possibility that Teresa had been the one to sneak back and push Ignazio to his death – although a ready motive still didn't occur to me. I tried another question. 'As far as Aldo's death is concerned, can you think of anybody who might have had a grudge against him?'

'It depends what you mean by grudge. If the stories about him were true – and I have no reason to believe they weren't – there were probably quite a few local women and their partners who disliked him. Whether this dislike was strong enough to translate itself into murder though, I seriously doubt.'

'And professionally? Did he have any arguments with staff, suppliers, neighbours?'

'Nothing I can think of. There were a few grumbles from staff – mainly about pay – and he had a row with the wine merchant the other day, but it wasn't exactly the kind of thing that leads to murder.'

I asked her if she had heard the name Ernesto Morso, the farmer who had allegedly been inveigled into selling his land to Aldo, but she just shook her head. 'That would all have been before my time. I've worked here for three years and the land had already been bought and developed by then. Sorry I can't help.'

She didn't look particularly sorry and as I left the office, I heard the volume of the music return to its former high pitch. I closed the door behind me and looked down at Oscar.

'She's a tough cookie, that one.'

The end of his tail started wagging. I had used the word 'cookie', after all.

15

TUESDAY EVENING

Back at the hotel, after a shower and a change of clothes, I went down to the terrace and found Virgilio and Inspector Fontana sitting at a table. Virgilio waved to me to join them, so I followed Oscar across and sat down.

'*Ciao*, Dan. What's new?'

'I've just been talking to Aldo Graziani's PA – or whatever she was. I must confess that I had been expecting at least some sort of display of emotion from her, but she seemed not just unmoved, but positively happy at the news of his death.' I glanced across at the inspector. 'I understand that you've already interviewed her. Was that your impression as well?'

Inspector Fontana nodded. 'Exactly the same. Of course, it might have been simply an attempt to quash the rumours of her and her boss carrying on, but if it was an act, she's a lot better than most of the people you see on the TV these days.' He produced a little smile. 'I understand from Virgilio that you're one of us – or at least you were. Chief Inspector makes you my superior officer, doesn't it?'

I heard that same note of regret beneath the good humour in his voice. Now that I knew about the effect of his injury on his career, I felt considerable sympathy for him. One of the reasons I'd taken early retirement at fifty-five had been because of rumours in the force that the powers that be were going to start moving frontline officers to desk work when they hit sixty, and I knew I would never have been able to put up with that. I smiled back at him.

'As Virgilio will have told you, I'm an *ex*-DCI now and I'm in the private sector. By the way, I don't want to butt into your investigation so I'm more than happy to go off and let you two talk shop if you prefer. I used to hate it when outsiders tried to horn in on my cases.'

'No, do stay and join us if you can spare the time. To be quite honest, I thought I recognised your name, so I had a word with a couple of colleagues in Pisa, and it seems you were very helpful in a case there not so long ago.' The waitress appeared and he waved to her. 'I'd like a cold beer, please.' He glanced at the two of us. 'Either of you feel like joining me?'

We did.

I asked him if he had received the pathologist's report, and his answer was interesting. 'It sounds very much like the same MO as his brother – a blow to the back of the head and then a push into the sea. His lungs weren't full of seawater, so there's no way he died of drowning. He was dead before he went in.'

'And presumably no sign of a murder weapon?' He shook his head and I asked him something else that had been preying on my mind. 'Do you have any information on the victim's will? Who inherits now that he's died?'

'As far as we can tell so far, he didn't have one. We've contacted his lawyer, who disclaims any knowledge of a will, and my people are searching his villa as we speak. I was there this afternoon and I couldn't see anything, but I've given orders that they have to check every scrap of paper they find. If he died intestate, it could take months or even years to decide on the settlement. Certainly, this hasn't thrown up any potential beneficiaries.'

This was disappointing. I'd been hoping to find somebody with a lot to gain from Aldo's death, but it looked as though this wasn't the case after all. 'Did he have any close relatives?'

'We've located his ex-wife, and the local police are interviewing her this evening, but she claims she hasn't seen or heard from the victim for three years or more. Otherwise, all we've found so far is a cousin living in

Livorno who says he hasn't spoken to either of the brothers for thirty years. It appears that they weren't a close family.'

The waitress returned with our drinks, and I waited until she'd left before continuing. 'Did you manage to locate the farmer, Ernesto Morso, who sold Aldo the land?'

'We've located him, but it didn't do us any good. He died two months ago. I've just spoken to his son, Fabio, on the phone, and he's going to call in here to see me any moment now. He lives not far from here.'

Only a few minutes later, as we were still discussing the case, a tall, slim man wearing full cycling gear appeared and stepped off a very smart, bright-yellow mountain bike. He rested it against a big, terracotta vase, climbed up the steps to the terrace and came over to our table. The inspector waved him into a seat, and I was in the process of getting up to leave them to it when Fontana shot me a quick smile and indicated for me to stay put. He shook hands with the new arrival, and we all sat down.

'Thank you for coming so quickly, Signor Morso. We'll try not to take too much of your time. We just have a few questions about your father and, in particular, his relationship with a man called Aldo Graziani.'

Fabio Morso pulled a couple of paper napkins out of the dispenser on the table and wiped the sweat off his brow. He was probably in his late forties, and he was wearing dark glasses. There was a serious expression on his face as he answered. 'Aldo Graziani was responsible for my father's death.'

The inspector raised an eyebrow. 'He killed your father?'

'In effect, yes.' Morso had an educated accent. 'Five years ago, Graziani forced my father to sell him a valuable piece of land – what is now Graziani's campsite just along the coast from here. It was a productive vineyard, and it had been my father's life's work to establish it and nurture it. I could hardly believe my ears when he told me he'd sold it. Ever since then, he's been on the decline, and he often said he had nothing left to live for. The official diagnosis was that he died of lung cancer two months ago, but I know it was of a broken heart.'

'When you say Aldo Graziani *forced* your father to sell, in what way? Are you talking about physical intimidation?'

Morso shook his head slowly. 'I honestly don't know the details – my father always refused to speak about it. I've been living in Rome for twelve years and I only come home every now and then. I travel a lot and in fact, I've spent most of the last three years living and working in Brazil. I'm a scientist. Under the circumstances, I didn't see my father that often and we didn't talk a lot, but I'm sure Graziani didn't subject him to physical violence. He would never have dared – my father was a big, strong man. It must have been some other form of coercion.'

'Such as?'

'I've been trying to work that out. My mother died eight years ago, but I've spoken to friends of my father here on the island as well as to my cousins who live in Santa Sabina, but nobody's been able to shed any light on it. Everybody agrees that the vineyard was my father's pride and joy, but the fact remains that he sold it to Graziani for a fraction of its true value.'

Virgilio and I exchanged glances. The word that was going through my mind was blackmail. It sounded as though Aldo Graziani had had some kind of hold over Ernesto Morso. If so, what might this have been?

The inspector continued with more questions, but without any further success. I kept a close eye on Fabio Morso as he answered and, although everything he said sounded clear and logical, for some reason – call it an old copper's hunch – I was left with the feeling that he hadn't told us everything. Could it be that he did know the true reason why his father had been blackmailed by Graziani, but had decided not to reveal it?

On the inspector's instructions, the waitress brought him a large glass of water and Morso drained it in one gulp. It was still a very hot day, and Elba certainly isn't a flat island. Presumably. he was a fit man to venture out on a bike. I asked him about his time in Brazil – more to let him talk, so I could get a better feel for the man – and he told us he was an anthropologist at La Sapienza, the famous university in Rome, and he had been studying the indigenous tribes of the Amazon. He said he was here for a few weeks' holiday and then he would be heading back to Rome to prepare for the new semester. He sounded sincere but I couldn't shake the feeling that he wasn't telling us everything.

After he had disappeared off to his bike, the three of us looked at each other for a few moments before Fontana commented. 'I have a feeling that gentleman knows why his father sold the land to Graziani. The fact that he isn't revealing this to us tells me it might be shame or embarrassment – maybe his father had a dirty little secret – but I'm convinced there's more to it than meets the eye. What did you two think?'

Virgilio nodded in agreement. 'To me, it sounds like Aldo Graziani was blackmailing his father, and I agree that the son probably knows what it was all about. He struck me as an intelligent man so he can have been under no illusions that not answering fully in a murder investigation could get him into trouble so, whatever it was, it must have been serious. What did you think, Dan?'

'I agree with both of you. I've just been doing a bit of calculating. Graziani bought the land five years ago. Around about the same time three other things happened: Tommaso Graziani, the two brothers' father, died; Aldo had the affair with a married woman which resulted in him getting a broken nose and effectively being banned from the village of Santa Sabina; and his wife divorced him. Could there be a link between any of these events and Aldo's death?' I looked across at the inspector. 'Did Virgilio tell you the story of Aldo's affair with Veronica Piccolo? Did you manage to track her down?'

'We're still looking. Sergeant Gallo's going to interview the woman's ex-husband this evening. Maybe he'll be able to shed some light. We'll ask him if anybody can confirm where he was and what he was doing last night, although it seems unlikely that he would have waited five years to murder Aldo. I suppose there might be a link, but it's tenuous.'

I had to agree. 'If it turns out that Aldo's ex-wife and the husband of Veronica Piccolo have alibis, that leaves us with Fabio Morso, who might have decided to take revenge now that his father has died. Alternatively, maybe it was a woman – like his ex-wife or Teresa the PA, for example. There's definitely something about her I don't trust.'

Fontana nodded in agreement. 'Sergeant Gallo feels sure the PA was having an affair with Aldo and he could well be right. Maybe they were together, but then it turned ugly and she took her revenge. I could see her being capable of committing murder.'

I brought up the other hypothesis. 'Of course, there's always the Etruscan connection. If Aldo was digging up and dealing in antiquities, might he have been killed for profit, by a rival, or even to shut him up? In a close-knit community like Santa Sabina, I find it hard to believe that he could have been carrying out archaeological excavations without somebody noticing. I wouldn't mind betting that he was the subject of the ongoing TPC investigation.'

Fontana nodded. 'That could well be true. I'll be speaking to the two *Carabinieri* officers later on, so I should know more by tonight. The fact is that both brothers managed to make themselves unpopular on the island. It strikes me there are a number of people who are going to be opening a bottle of *spumante* tonight to celebrate the death of this brother, just as I'm sure a lot of people were glad to see Ignazio meet his death.'

We carried on talking and Inspector Fontana asked for my help. 'First thing tomorrow morning, I'd like to interview all of the guests here at the hotel. As far as I can see from the file, they've only had token interviews so far, just checking where they were at the time of the first death. I'd like to know more about them. Some of them speak Italian but others don't. Virgilio tells me that you've helped him in the past with interpreting and, as my English is non-existent, if you could spare the time from your windsurfing course to help out for an hour or so, I'd be very grateful.'

'My course doesn't start till ten-thirty so maybe before that? But either way, I'd be pleased to help. I can be available any time.' Hopefully, Anna would forgive me yet again for allowing police work to interfere with our holiday.

He thanked me and told me he would arrange the interviews with the non-Italian speakers to begin at nine o'clock so I could get off to my course in good time.

I was looking forward to the opportunity of speaking to the guests who were, after all, still potential suspects in the death of the first brother. As for the second murder, it was clear that Aldo Graziani hadn't been that much more popular than his brother, but it was hard to see why anybody should have waited five years to kill him if his death was somehow related to his womanising past or his divorce. Hopefully, good solid police work, interviewing suspects and checking their stories would provide us with some answers because, for the moment, I didn't have any.

Apart from anything else, we still had no idea whether we were looking for one murderer or two.

16

TUESDAY NIGHT

Tuesday night turned out to be pizza night, and it was another outstanding meal. It started with mixed seafood antipasti ranging from little skewers of grilled prawns and baby octopus to grilled anchovies with an unusual, orange-flavoured coating, and clams in a spicy tomato sauce. Anna and Lina expressed delight, and Oscar had a smile on his face after being handed down his share of prawn heads and other titbits. I ate heartily. Windsurfing, I had already discovered, not only made your shoulders ache; it also did wonders for the appetite.

As we ate, I told Anna and the others about my walk in the abandoned vineyard and my discovery of the slag heaps indicating the presence of mines dating back several thousand years. Anna was very interested, and we agreed that I would take her up there the following day when our afternoon windsurfing session finished. I asked Virgilio what he intended to do the next day, and I was pleased to hear him say that he and Lina were planning on driving around the island. This week was supposed to be a holiday for the two of them and it was good to see that he was managing to switch off a bit, now that there was a more committed investigating officer in charge of the case.

We were sitting at our usual table, and from my seat, I had a good view of the other guests. Presumably, news of the second death must have filtered through to everybody by now – along with the instruction not to leave the hotel – and there was a distinct air of apprehension. As ever, the only ones who seemed indifferent to the drama were the young newly-weds at the far end of the terrace, still totally absorbed in each other's company. I caught sight of Tatsuo, alone at his table as usual, and he toasted me with his glass of beer. I picked up my glass and toasted him back, reflecting that my windsurfing prowess was as good as his now – well, almost.

Tonight, the Graziani table was empty, and my mind flitted back to Ignazio's death. Over the past couple of days, I had definitely been coming around to believing that he'd been killed by his brother, but Aldo's recent murder threw that hypothesis into doubt. While it was still possible, the similarity in the modus operandi of the two murders made me tend to think that we were probably looking at a single killer. The great unknown was why both brothers should have been targeted. Although I was looking forward to interviewing the hotel guests with the inspector in the morning, I was still convinced that there had to be a local connection. A thought occurred to me and I leant forward to talk to Virgilio while Lina and Anna were still discussing Etruscan history.

'Did you or Piero Fontana have any joy with the staff here at the hotel? Might one of them have had a run-in with the Graziani brothers?'

'Nothing that leapt out at us. The chef's only been here for two years and he's originally from south of Rome. The cleaning staff are a Romanian and a Nigerian, and the only people with a solid local connection are the waiter, the waitress, the night porter and, of course, Rita.'

'What about the owner of the hotel, Alfonso Silvano? Presumably, he's a local, isn't he?'

'Yes, indeed, but I think we can safely eliminate him from our inquiries. Rita tells me he's a sick man. He suffers from emphysema – caused by too much smoking – and just walking from here to the clifftop involves him stopping two or three times for a rest. There's no way he could have climbed out of a window, sneaked through the trees and assaulted the first victim, let alone the second. As for the two cleaning staff, I think they're also almost certainly in the clear because I can't even begin to think of a motive. The assistant chef only arrived from Milan a month ago and he would appear to have no connection with the island. He's only just eighteen and, from what Rita said, assistant chef is rather a grand title for the general kitchen dogsbody who does everything from chopping the carrots to washing the dishes.'

'So that leaves us with the chef, the waiter, the waitress, the night porter and Rita.'

'Antonio and Annamaria, the serving staff, are reported to be a happily married couple who live in the village. They've worked here at the hotel for seven years now and Rita speaks very highly of them. She herself has worked here for over ten years and I can't see any of the three having a motive to suddenly decide to murder either or both victims. The chef is a Roman with no connections to the island, so he doesn't strike me as suspicious either, so that just leaves us with Elvis, the night porter.'

'Elvis, really?' I couldn't help smiling. 'Not the commonest of Italian names.'

Virgilio smiled. 'I imagine his parents were fans of the great man. I haven't had a chance to speak to him, but Piero says he's going to see him tomorrow, along with all the staff and guests. If Piero doesn't mind, I might sit in alongside him. It would appear that Inspector Bellini only gave the staff a cursory interview, so there may be more to dig up. Elvis is also a local and he's worked here for a year, but what's interesting is that he previously worked at the Grazianis' campsite for years, first for the father and then for Aldo. This means that he knew Aldo well, so let's see if he can add anything to the inquiry.'

'And there's no connection between any of the guests and the four women assaulted by Ignazio in Pisa?'

'Not a trace.' There was a frustrated expression on his face as he reached for his glass, and I knew how he felt.

Anna was still talking to Lina, so I sat back and took a good look around. The four Brits seemed fairly happy, if a bit more subdued than previous nights. There was just about enough light left for me to get a better look at them and it seemed to me that they were probably around my age or a bit older, two men and two women. It was hard to tell in the twilight, but from the necklaces sparkling in the flickering candlelight, I got the feeling they were probably well-off tourists who had deliberately chosen the island and this hotel as an alternative to the more crowded resorts on the mainland.

Just beyond them, I noted that Signor Giardino from Lucca and his wife barely exchanged a single word. Marco had said that they were shop-keepers, and I wondered whether they had just shut up shop while they came on holiday, or whether somebody else was looking after it for them. Of course, for all I knew, they might own a supermarket and have a whole infrastructure of staff looking after the business while they were away.

The Swiss divers, Heidi and Martin, were talking to each other but they, too, looked apprehensive. Murder can do that to people. I wondered idly whether they had come across any Etruscan artefacts on the seabed. I had read an article online about somebody discovering a beautifully preserved statue dating back to Roman times about ten metres down just off the north coast of the island. Thought of this set me thinking once again of the story the *Carabinieri* officer had told about the illegal trade in antiquities, and at that very moment, the two officers appeared on the steps to the terrace.

They stopped as they passed our table. The red-haired one gave a polite nod to the four of us and bent low to murmur quietly in Virgilio's ear before following his companion along to their table. Once they had gone, I gave Virgilio an inquiring look.

'Anything exciting?'

'Apparently, they've been given orders to return to the mainland tomorrow to question a pair of *tombaroli* accused of unearthing Etruscan remains not far from Populonia. After that, they're on their way back to Rome.'

'I wonder whether this means that the death of Aldo Graziani marks the end of their involvement here on the island. The more I think about it, the more I'm convinced he was their target all along. Presumably, now that he's dead, there's no point in staying.'

Virgilio shrugged his shoulders. 'Who knows? Piero said he was going to interview them this evening so he might have found out a bit more. I definitely got the feeling they were keeping their cards pretty close to their chests when I spoke to them yesterday, so you might be right about Aldo.'

I turned this possible connection around in my head a few times. If

Aldo had indeed been dealing in illegal antiquities, who had murdered him? Surely not the two *Carabinieri*, but, if not, then who? And, even if his death had been linked to the illegal antiquities trade, why had Ignazio been killed? There was no way he could have had anything to do with digging up Etruscan artefacts from inside prison, so had his death been a straight case of mistaken identity, or was I missing something significant?

When the waiter came around with the pizza menu, I was impressed to see quite a choice of different toppings on offer as well as the more common ones like *margherita* and *quattro stagioni*. Anna opted for one called *tartufella*, which was a mixture of burrata cheese, white truffle cream, mortadella and crushed pistachio nuts. As we were by the seaside, I chose the house special *pizza ai frutti di mare* and, when it arrived, I could barely see any of the base beneath a mountain of prawns, clams, mussels, octopus and squid rings. With perfectly cooked, thin dough it tasted as good as it looked.

I would like to be able to report that I had the strength of character not to allow myself to be tempted by the dessert menu but I told myself I was on holiday and, besides, falling into the sea and climbing back out again on a regular basis was surely burning off a healthy number of calories, so I opted for homemade apricot tart and ice cream.

By the time we reached the end of our meal, and coffees were served, I could definitely say that this had been one of the best meals I had ever had. At my feet, Oscar was also sporting a satisfied canine smile after subjecting Lina to his most convincing *Dan doesn't feed me* look that had resulted in him bagging a generous selection of titbits – plus, of course, some bits of pizza crust from me, as per our long-standing agreement.

After dinner, Anna and I took Oscar for a walk and, although I felt sure he would have loved a trip to the beach and the chance to go swimming again, the idea of sharing our room tonight with a soggy dog didn't appeal to either of us, so we headed inland as far as the village and walked around the handful of narrow streets. I could well understand how in a little place like this, everybody would know everybody, and the presence of a predatory character like Ignazio Graziani – or, indeed, his brother – would have aroused indignation or more in the whole community. Once again, I wondered about the story of the attempted abduction twenty years earlier.

If locals like the barista or Rita couldn't confirm it, then I tended to believe that it most probably hadn't happened. In all likelihood, it had been invented by somebody to embellish the exploits of the mob who had gone to old Signor Graziani's house to insist that he banish his younger son from the island.

Although it was barely ten o'clock, the bar in the piazza was already closed and the dark streets were deserted. Night had fallen, the temperature had dropped a few degrees, and I felt sure most people were hunkered down trying to get some sleep before yet another hot day tomorrow. I did my best to switch off my detective brain for a few minutes and concentrated on absorbing the stimuli coming in from all around me. Although we were here on an island and the book I was writing was set well inland, I felt sure I could include the flickering of fireflies in the branches of trees, the heady scent of wisteria and the distant hooting of an owl when writing night scenes in and around San Gimignano. My editor was always telling me to be as descriptive as possible, so I did my best to soak up all the sounds and scents and try to find the right words to describe the interplay of the moonlight and the shadows. The bad news was that my current problem wasn't with description; it was with the plot itself. I had a dead body lying at the bottom of a high tower and I had no idea who had caused the death. I was hoping that the fact that this was not dissimilar to the Graziani murders would help me, but until we solved those, I remained stuck. I was still thinking about this when we returned to the hotel and went to bed.

We were woken in the middle of the night by a flash of lightning that lit up the room, almost immediately followed by a clap of thunder that rattled the open windows and roused Oscar from dreams of swimming in the sea and prawn heads. He got up from his position on the cool, ceramic tiles by the bed and padded over to rest his nose on the mattress alongside me, his eyes glowing green in the moonlight. Outside the window, a torrential deluge came pouring down, sounding more like a waterfall than raindrops, accompanied by powerful gusts of wind that made the windows swing wildly. I reached out and gave Oscar's head a reassuring stroke while my mind inevitably returned once again to the two mysterious deaths. Two highly unpopular brothers had been murdered in the same way within a few days of each other and everything was crying out to me to say that it had been the work of a single killer. There had to be something that linked them, but what could that be?

I was still pondering this when the worst of the storm finally passed over us and the rain stopped as suddenly as it had started, although I could hear the wind continue to blow. I felt Anna stir and turn towards me.

'How wonderful. It feels so much cooler.'

'It certainly does.' I rolled over towards her as Oscar subsided onto the floor beside the bed once more. 'Well, how are you enjoying your holiday so far?'

She smiled. 'I've just been lying here calculating that if I'd chosen a boyfriend with an interest in fashion, I'd probably have a wardrobe full of the very latest styles by now. It seems to me that every time we try and go on holiday together, you suddenly turn back into a detective again.' I was about to apologise when she reached up and laid a calming hand against my cheek. 'It's all right, *carissimo*, I understand, really, I do. The instinct's stronger than you are, I know. It's just like Oscar chasing squirrels. It's in your DNA and it will never leave you.' She gave me a kiss. 'It's a shame I haven't ended up with a wardrobe full of beautiful clothes, but that's life, and I wouldn't want you any other way.'

17

WEDNESDAY MORNING

The wind was blowing a lot harder when I got up next morning and took Oscar for his walk. On the coast, it was hard enough to bend the branches of the trees, and there were big rollers coming in, throwing up clouds of white spray as they pounded against the rocks. I had a sinking feeling that today's windsurfing lesson might turn into an outing for the local lifeboat – with me the object of their attentions.

When I got to the windsurfing school, I saw Ingrid and Stefano standing on the terrace drinking coffee, and she gave me the news I had secretly been hoping to hear.

'*Ciao*, Dan, we've just been talking and we think it's best if we cancel today's lessons. With an offshore wind and such big waves, it's a recipe for disaster. We'll make the hours up over the next few days. We're very sorry, but we think it's the sensible thing to do.'

I decided to tell them the truth. 'I must confess that I feel relieved. I don't think I'm qualified for waves this size and I certainly wouldn't want to get washed away. Are you cancelling Anna's class as well?'

Stefano nodded. 'Tell her she can come and try if she likes, but I have a feeling she'll find it too much like hard work.'

Ingrid agreed. 'And potentially dangerous. How about a coffee?'

I glanced at my watch. It was still barely seven-thirty and Anna was probably only just thinking about getting up, so I thanked her and asked for an espresso. While she went in to get it, I had a word with Stefano about his beloved Etruscans.

'I took Oscar for a walk in the field you told me about yesterday afternoon and managed to see quite a few overgrown slag heaps left over from ancient mines. I'm sure you're right and there must have been a settlement around here somewhere. I couldn't find a smelting furnace either, but I did look for it.' I went on to tell him about the spring and my theory that it might have marked the site of a settlement and he looked interested, but I added a proviso. 'But you'll probably need to come back in the winter because for now, everything is submerged under the vines. Do you happen to know who owns the field?'

He produced an ironic smile. 'I'm not sure who it belongs to now, but it used to belong to Aldo Graziani when he was alive.'

'Was he was planning on expanding the campsite up there?'

'Anything's possible, I don't know. I believe he bought it at the same time as he bought the fields where the campsite is now.'

'The field looks abandoned and the track's overgrown. All I could see was a big shed up there. Was that his as well?'

'I imagine so. It appeared just after I started here four summers ago and in fact, the remains of the *fabbrichile* are just beyond it but, like you say, they're virtually inaccessible underneath all the plants at this time of year. I'm not sure if he ever used the shed. I have a feeling it might have been a planning scam – you know, pretending there's been a building there for years and then asking for permission to build another to replace that one and building a villa instead. That's the sort of sneaky character he was. I don't think there's anything in the shed. I've never seen him or anybody else going in there, so I bet it was some sort of fiddle.'

Ingrid reappeared carrying a little cup of coffee for me and half a ham sandwich for Oscar. 'Somebody left this here last night and I kept it because I thought Oscar might like it. Can I give it to him?'

He nodded before I did.

As I sipped my coffee, I thought I would do a little bit of digging. 'You come back every summer, don't you, Stefano? What about you, Ingrid? Do you work here all year round?'

She nodded. 'I live and work here all year round, but I'm not as busy out of season as I am in the summer.'

'Do you live at the campsite?'

'No, I live in Santa Sabina with Maria, my partner. I've been coming here on holiday with my parents every summer for as long as I can remember, and Maria and I first met as teenagers. We stayed friends even though we drifted apart, but then I came back and we set up home together a couple of years ago.'

'And what about Maria? Was she a holidaymaker like you and your family, or is she originally from here?'

'She's a local. Her parents own the shop in the main piazza and she works there.'

This was sounding promising. Presumably, the bar, the church and the only shop were the hubs of the little village and, hopefully, the fount of all knowledge about what went on around here. I decided to put my cards on the table. 'I used to be in the police in the UK and I now have my own investigation agency in Florence.' I saw them both look up at me with increased interest. 'I'm helping the police investigate the two recent murders and I wonder if you could help me.'

Stefano answered first. 'So they were definitely both murdered? I heard that Aldo's brother got drunk and fell off the cliff.'

'That's still possible, but with this second death – and this one was definitely murder, there's no doubt about it – it seems like too much of a coincidence. I believe they were *both* murdered and I'm also pretty sure there has to be a local connection. I was talking to some of the people in the village the other day and they mentioned an attempted abduction of a girl twenty years ago, apparently by Ignazio Graziani. Does that ring any bells with you?'

They both shook their heads and Ingrid replied. 'I'm sorry but twenty years ago, I would only have been seven. I can ask Maria's parents if you like. They've lived here all their lives and if anybody knows, they will.'

'Thank you, that would be very helpful.'

Stefano was looking at me closely. 'When Teresa was down here yesterday, she told me she thought you were a detective. If you're a private investigator, does this mean that somebody has employed you to look into these deaths?'

I launched into a cover story that wasn't too far from the truth. 'No, this was supposed to be my week off, but seeing as the police have instructed all the guests at the Augustus to stay put, I thought I'd do a bit of sniffing around of my own in the hope of speeding up the investigation.'

At that moment, I spotted Teresa by the entrance to the beach. She was chatting animatedly to a couple of holidaymakers, and from time to time, I heard peals of laughter from them. She was wearing short shorts and a bright primrose-yellow top and she looked as though she hadn't got a care in the world. Certainly, if she and Aldo had been having an affair, she appeared to have got over his loss remarkably easily – suspiciously easily. I watched as the three of them disappeared back up the track to the campsite before resuming my questions to Stefano and Ingrid.

'Could you tell me in confidence anything you know about Teresa that might be of interest to me? Where's she from? Was she telling me the truth when she said she and Aldo didn't have a romantic liaison? Anything that might help would be great.'

Ingrid was the first to reply. 'I honestly can't make her out. She's very organised and she can be extremely smiley and helpful when she wants, but there's something about her that unsettles me. Whether she had an affair with Aldo or not – and I tend to think that she did – I never sensed any kind of deep emotional attachment between the two of them. She started working here three years ago and she's definitely made the place more efficient. I'm sure the campers like her but, like I say, deep down, she's quite a tough character.' She glanced across at Stefano. 'You get on reasonably well with her, don't you, Stefano?'

I saw him cast a wary look around before answering. 'I suppose so but, like you say, Ingrid, she's a difficult person to connect with. To be honest, the only thing Teresa and I have in common is ancient history. Since coming to the island, she's become very interested in the Etruscans, so we sometimes sit down and talk about them. She doesn't seem to have many friends – well, she doesn't seem to have *any* friends around here really. She keeps herself to herself and I think she has her own agenda, and she doesn't share it with anyone.'

I sipped my coffee and mulled over in my head what I'd just heard.
What might Teresa's secret agenda be, and did her interest in the Etruscans
point towards her possibly being involved with the illicit antiquities trade?
I hoped the inspector had been able to dig up something interesting in her
background. Might she have come here with a sinister purpose? The fact
was, however, that she had arrived here three years ago, so why wait until
now if she had been planning to murder her boss? Or had she been waiting
until the brother was released from prison so that she could murder both
of them? Frustratingly, yet again, the question was why.

* * *

I had the opportunity to mention Teresa to the inspector at nine o'clock
that morning when I joined him and Sergeant Gallo in a downstairs room
at the hotel for the interviews. I was pleased to see that Virgilio had
decided to go off and spend some time with Lina. It's tough enough being
the wife of a police officer without work encroaching on holidays. It looked
as though he had finally remembered that he was on holiday – although it
occurred to me that I was a fine one to talk. In answer to my question about
Aldo's PA, Fontana checked the file on the desk in front of him and his
reply was interesting, if inconclusive.

'Here's what we know about her so far: Teresa Franceschini, age
thirty-seven, unmarried. Originally from Padua, where she went to
school and attended university. Worked as a tourist guide for one of the
big international tour companies until she took up the job here on the
island three years ago. No criminal record, not even an outstanding
parking ticket.' He looked up. 'Nothing suspicious there, but, like you
two, I feel sure there's more to her than meets the eye. We'll see how
this morning's interviews go, but if we don't get any joy out of the
people here, I'm going to sit down and talk to Teresa Franceschini
again later on. I might even take her to the station and let her sweat a
bit.'

I turned to Sergeant Gallo. 'Sergeant, did you get any joy from the
husband of the woman who had the affair with Aldo?'

'Veronica Piccolo – the husband had an address for her in Buenos

Aires, so we contacted the Argentine police. They confirm that she's still there, so no chance of her having sneaked back here to kill Aldo.'

I shrugged. 'There goes another lead.'

* * *

The first interview didn't take long. It was with Tatsuo Tanaka from Nagoya, Japan. He told us he was thirty-five years old and a graphic designer. Apart from his telling us that he enjoyed travelling and had visited over a dozen countries – as confirmed by the stamps in his passport – there appeared to be nothing even vaguely suspicious about him, so Fontana soon thanked him and sent him away.

The four Brits were next, and Piero Fontana interviewed the first couple together. These were a Mr and Mrs Downing, both in their late sixties, who gave an address in Chelsea. I recognised the name of the street as one of the poshest in an already very posh – and astronomically expensive – part of London. I mentioned this in Italian to the inspector and he asked me to ask them what they did for a living. Mr Downing – 'call me Cyril' – told us he was the owner of an art gallery not far from Harrods department store. As far as these two were concerned, it was evident that money wasn't a problem, and we could find no connection between them and the Graziani brothers. As a result, that interview didn't last long either.

The other couple were Professor Walter and Dr Marguerite Scott, and they also lived in London – in their case in Harrow, which is a little further out of town, but highly desirable. From the point of view of the investigation, I was fascinated when he told us what he did for a living.

'I'm head of the department of pre-Roman studies at the University of London. My speciality is Etruscology – that's the study of the Etruscans. I'm sure you know that they formerly populated Etruria, the area that now comprises parts of central Italy, in particular Tuscany and Lazio, including here on the island of Elba.'

As I translated for the inspector's benefit, I caught his eye and saw him raise his eyebrows. Was this just coincidence or might the professor's purpose here be more than just a holiday? Piero Fontana clearly thought this significant as his next question implied.

'That's very interesting, Professor. I wonder if you could tell me how much you know about the trade in illegal antiquities here in Italy.'

If Professor Scott was surprised by the question, he didn't show it. 'A very grubby business, as I know to my cost. Three years ago, I was involved in a major archaeological dig a little way south of here on the mainland near Vulci. Like all archaeology, it was painstaking work, uncovering two-thousand-year-old relics millimetre by millimetre, using paintbrushes and hand trowels. Then, in the course of one night, tomb robbers swooped in, and next morning, we were faced with trenches over a metre deep, exhibiting the imprints of where large relics had been uncovered and spirited away. To this day, I have no idea exactly what was there, but you can be sure that the robbers made a lot of money out of selling whatever it was they found.'

'Are you aware of anything similar happening here? I believe Elba was an important island for the Etruscans.'

'Indeed it was, principally for its deposits of iron ore, but I'm not aware of any significant finds or reported losses from this area. Why? Have you uncovered something?'

Fontana ignored the question. 'So you're saying that you don't think it likely that this particular part of the island might have produced valuable Etruscan remains?'

'As far as I'm aware, there would have been mining communities on the island, but I don't think there would have been anything of any great artistic value to a collector.'

After he and his wife had been thanked and dismissed, Piero Fontana shook his head slowly. 'Everything keeps coming back to the Etruscans. Could it really be that either or both of the murders have a connection with people who lived here over two thousand years ago?'

I had been thinking along the very same lines. 'Did you have a chance to speak to the two *Carabinieri* officers last night? Did they have anything to add to what they already told you?'

'A bit, yes. Although the trafficker in illegal antiquities that the TPC have under arrest in Bologna still claims never to have known the name of his contact in Tuscany, he apparently let slip at some point that the object had been found on the island of Elba, on land near a campsite not far from

Porto Azzurro. The Graziani establishment isn't the only one in this area but it's one of the biggest, and these two officers confirmed that they had been keeping Aldo under observation. Now that he's been killed, the trail here has gone cold, so that's why they're moving on.'

I digested what he'd told me and felt ever more convinced that Aldo's recently found wealth stemmed from his discovery of Etruscan remains – possibly with the assistance of his PA with an interest in ancient history. I was about to voice a hypothesis that I'd been turning over in my head for a while, when he said it for me.

'What about this suggestion? Let's assume for the moment that Aldo managed to lay his hands on some valuable pieces of Etruscan art. It's highly unlikely that he would have been able to identify and contact a major trafficker or potential buyers overseas, so he would almost certainly have looked for a handler here in Tuscany. Whoever that handler is, it's probably safe to say that he or she is the one who dealt with the man currently in custody in Bologna. The Tuscan handler knows that it's probably only a matter of time before the trafficker in Bologna gives him away and so he decides to take action to eliminate one of the only other people who knows his identity – and that person was Aldo.'

I was impressed. Fontana's thought process was very similar to my own, but I thought I'd better mention the fly in the ointment that had already occurred to me. 'It's an interesting theory, and it's something I've been turning over in my head, but there's a problem and you've just said it yourself. You said that Aldo was *one* of the people who knew the identity of the handler, so there would have been others. This as yet unidentified person was a go-between, and his name would have been known to a number of local *tombaroli*. Unless you're aware of reports of other suspicious deaths in this area in the last few days, there would have been little point in this guy murdering Aldo unless he was trying to kill off all his contacts, and I can't see that as viable.'

I saw Piero Fontana nod in agreement. 'Point taken. And that makes it less likely that his murder was tied up with the illegal antiquity trade.'

I had also been thinking about this. 'Yes and no. Although I don't think it's very likely that Aldo was murdered by the local handler, he might well have been murdered by a competitor or even a partner here on the island.

With big money to be made, it's possible that somebody might have decided to kill him off so as to get a bigger share. Which brings us back to Teresa Franceschini. Was her connection with him a business rather than a romantic partnership? Might she have killed him so as to get her hands on everything?'

Piero Fontana exchanged glances with the sergeant. 'Gallo, you and I definitely need to sit down and have a long, hard talk with Teresa Franceschini. Maybe her relationship with Aldo was both a business *and* a romantic partnership and, like Dan says, she killed him either so as to get her hands on the buried treasure, or out of jealousy, or for other, more personal reasons. The problem is that I can't see what motive she might have had to murder the brother, Ignazio. There's surely no way she could have confused the two of them, even in the dark. If she killed Aldo, maybe somebody else killed Ignazio. Either way, I'm increasingly suspicious of her and we definitely need to lean on her hard.'

The last interview with which I was involved was with the Swiss couple. They told us that they had been coming back here every summer for four years because they loved the place. Heidi told us she worked for the Swiss post office while Martin, her fiancé, worked in a bank. They disclaimed any knowledge of either of the brothers and told us that they had been in their room when both deaths had occurred. The inspector thanked them and, after they had left, he pointed out that none of the hotel guests could provide alibis for the times of either killing apart from the word of their partner or spouse, which, of course, in a court of law meant little or nothing. Basically, we found ourselves with a lot of suspects without alibis, but without any appreciable motive.

I glanced down at Oscar, who was stretched out on the floor at my feet. Sensing that he was being observed, he opened one eye but then let his eyelid drop once again. Clearly, we weren't going to get any suggestions out of him.

18

WEDNESDAY MORNING

Seeing that our windsurfing lessons had been cancelled, Anna and I decided to walk up to the overgrown field so that she could see the remains of the Etruscan mines that Stefano had mentioned. It was actually quite hard work walking inland into the face of the gusty wind, but I felt a whole lot safer than if I had been out on a surfboard. Here on dry land, the breeze made a very pleasant and refreshing change from the unrelenting heat of the previous days.

We crossed the road and walked up the track as far as Aldo Graziani's shed. Close up, this was a relatively large building, and, as Stefano had said, it looked deserted. While Anna and Oscar fought their way into the undergrowth looking for signs of the Etruscan mines or smelting furnaces, I examined the wooden shed more closely. The first thing that struck me was that there were no recent tyre marks or footprints leading to it. Clearly, it had not been used for some considerable length of time. The other thing that struck me was that the front doors were secured by a high-security lock – one of those expensive ones that has a long, flat key, like the lock on the outside door of my office. If the shed was empty, this seemed excessive, and if there was something inside, it was clear it was something of value. My detective antennae started twitching and I walked around all four sides of the building, looking to see if there might be any other way in. But I looked in vain.

Unable to satisfy my curiosity, I waited in the shade for several minutes until Anna appeared, sweating profusely and looking disappointed. 'Without a flamethrower, we don't stand a chance of finding anything underneath all this greenery.'

To emphasise her point, Oscar appeared behind her with a long piece of vine that had somehow got tangled up in his collar and was now trailing behind him like a second tail. As I bent down and removed it, I pointed out the security lock.

'I have a feeling there might be something valuable in here. I'll report this to the inspector and hopefully, his people will be able to locate the key.'

She looked more animated. 'What do you think's in here? Wouldn't it be amazing if we found a load of Etruscan artefacts?'

Secretly, this was what I was hoping as well, but I decided to temper my expectations and hers – at least for now – so I avoided speculating. I pulled out my phone and called Piero Fontana. He answered immediately and I told him where I was and voiced my suspicions. He told me he was still interviewing the hotel guests but promised to send somebody to the camp-site reception desk to ask Teresa for the keys. I wished him luck, but I had a feeling the keys wouldn't be there. Something was telling me that they wouldn't be found hanging on a hook. If the contents of the shed were what I was hoping, the keys were most probably hidden away somewhere very secure – like in a safe. Unless, of course, they had already been taken from Aldo Graziani's pockets after his death.

Anna and I walked into the centre of Santa Sabina and stopped at the café where the walls of the little church sheltered the tables from the wind. There were only two other people sitting outside and I recognised them as fellow guests at the hotel: the shopkeepers from Lucca. The man looked up and gave me a nod of the head while his wife had hers buried in her phone. As usual, they didn't appear to be speaking to each other, but maybe after thirty or forty years of marriage, they had exhausted all topics of conversation. I found myself wondering if they were enjoying them-selves. Even before the death of Ignazio, they had looked distinctly troubled, and my first impression of the man when I had seen him running up the path from the beach had been very different from what I would have expected of an average holidaymaker. What, I wondered, was bothering them?

We ordered coffees and chatted quietly as we drank. In spite of Anna's declaration that she didn't mind my unfortunate habit of getting involved with investigations at the most inconvenient times, I tried to keep my mind off the two recent deaths, and we talked about all sorts including, inevitably, the people who had inhabited the island two and a half thousand years ago.

My resolve didn't last long. In spite of my best intentions, an idea struck me as we were talking. I had been wondering how Aldo Graziani had been able to force Ernesto Morso to sell him his vineyard for a song, what he could have used to blackmail him, and it occurred to me that Aldo might have discovered Morso doing something illegal.

Might the illegal activity have involved Etruscan antiquities? What if Aldo had caught old Signor Morso digging up and disposing of valuable antiquities? In return for not shopping him to the police, Aldo had been able to get the land for a bargain price and then, as a canny businessman, had carried on the very lucrative antiquities trade for his own purposes. Might that be it?

The more I thought about it, the more the old vineyard and the unexpectedly large shed struck me as being pivotal to the investigation, and I was interested to find that Anna had apparently been thinking along the same lines as she looked up from her drink with a pensive expression on her face. 'I'm sure there's something valuable inside that shed and I'm equally sure that it's got something to do with the illicit antiquities trade. When do you think the inspector will be able to get hold of the key?'

'Probably in the next hour or so, as soon as he finishes the interviews at the hotel.'

'What if he can't find the key?'

'Very simple. His officers will force the doors open.'

Our conversation was interrupted by my phone. It was Virgilio. 'Dan, Marco has just sent me some fascinating information. Where are you at the moment?'

'I'm at the bar in the village.'

'Can you spare the time to come back to the hotel? I'm on my way there now to speak to Piero Fontana.'

I glanced across at Anna. 'It's Virgilio. Sounds like he's onto something. Do you feel like coming back to the hotel with me?'

After a brief pause, she gave me her answer. 'If it's all right with you, I think I'll go back to that overgrown field and do a bit more searching in the undergrowth. Shall I take Oscar with me for another walk?'

Her use of the magic word 'walk' was enough to get him on his feet, tail wagging in anticipation, so we headed off in different directions.

I made it back to the hotel in less than ten minutes and almost bumped into Virgilio by the front door. Together, we walked through to where Fontana was carrying out his interviews and waited until the door opened and Sergeant Gallo showed a young man out. At first, I didn't recognise the man's face but then realised that up till now I had only ever seen it pressed up close against his wife's. Evidently, he was Mr Arnaldo, half of the amorous couple of newly-weds.

Virgilio didn't waste time. 'Is the inspector free? I have some new information that I feel sure he'll be very interested to hear.'

Sergeant Gallo opened the door wide, and we went inside. Piero Fontana looked up and must have seen the excitement on Virgilio's face. '*Ciao*, Virgilio, what's new?'

'You know I said I've got my people in Florence checking up on Ignazio's original assault and rape cases? Well, I've just heard back, and two things have come up. The second woman to be abducted by Ignazio Graziani, Laura Bracco, has an Italian father, but her mother is originally Japanese, and, of all places, she comes from Nagoya. It strikes me as quite a coincidence that we have a man here at the hotel from that very same city. I think we might need to find out more about Tatsuo Tanaka. Who knows, he might be a relative of the mother or even a professional hitman?'

Inspector Fontana looked very interested and immediately ordered the sergeant to contact the Japanese police to see whether they had anything on Tanaka, but Virgilio's news didn't stop there.

'There's more. The couple of shopkeepers, Signor Giardino and his wife from Lucca, run a very specialised sort of shop. It's an antique shop, but what's special about it is that the website claims it boasts a large collection of "ancient artefacts, some dating back to pre-Roman times.". Again, that's quite a coincidence, isn't it?'

Fontana nodded ruefully. 'I interviewed them an hour ago, but I didn't ask what sort of shop they had. All they told me was that they were here on holiday.' He returned his attention to the sergeant. 'Could you call them back in, please, Gallo? Hopefully, they're still around.'

I pointed out that I'd just seen them at the café in the village and the sergeant went out to send somebody for them. I looked back at Virgilio. 'Suddenly, we might have a suspect for the first murder – a revenge killing all the way from Japan – and another for Aldo's murder, this time connected to the antiques trade. Maybe we aren't looking for a single killer after all.'

I saw the other two exchange glances and I felt a distinct ripple of optimism run through the room. Might one of these snippets of information be the breakthrough we had been seeking?

At that moment, I heard scratching at the door, accompanied by a familiar bark. I jumped to my feet as a young constable opened the door and Oscar came charging in. The officer looked at the inspector apologetically.

'I'm sorry, sir, but this dog won't go away. We keep shooing it off, but it keeps coming back. I don't suppose—'

I interrupted him to reassure him that Oscar was known to me and I looked around for Anna. Unable to see her, I checked with the constable. His answer was disconcerting.

'No, sir, the dog was on its own. The officer out front said it came running up the drive and onto the terrace before coming in here. There was nobody with it.'

My brain was racing. If Oscar had come all the way here by himself, this meant he had run along the main road. This had been potentially dangerous to him but, more to the point, I found myself wondering desperately why Anna wasn't with him. As I stroked his head to calm him down, I turned back to Virgilio and Piero.

'I'm worried something's happened to Anna. She went off to the field with the shed again. I need to get back there now.'

Virgilio was already on his feet. 'I'll come with you.' He glanced back at
the inspector. 'Can you spare us a couple of officers? I don't like the sound
of this.'

Together with Sergeant Gallo and the young constable, we raced out of
the hotel and back out of the gate, along the road to the field. We followed
Oscar up the overgrown track, but when we approached the shed, I could
see no sign of Anna, and I found my anxiety levels rising. It had been quite
out of character for Oscar to run off on his own, and I felt sure he would
only have done so if something serious had happened. What was immediately apparent was that Oscar had no doubt that the answer to the puzzle
lay inside the shed. With his nose firmly positioned by the crack of the
door, he stood up on his hind legs and started desperately scratching with
his front paws.

Virgilio and I exchanged glances and he turned to the two police officers. 'We need to get into this shed now. See if you can break the doors
down or look for something we can use to lever them open.'

The two officers shoulder-charged the doors and I heard the timber
give a creak of protest. Virgilio and I joined in and with a series of
concerted efforts – and a few bruised shoulders – we managed to split the
wood around the lock until the right-hand door swung out on its hinges.
We ran inside and stopped in surprise. Apart from an aluminium ladder
hanging on one wall, the shed was empty.

This wasn't what I had been expecting. Virgilio and I were exchanging
bewildered looks when my eyes were drawn to Oscar. He had run past us
and was now scratching frantically at the floor of the shed in the far corner.
I rushed after him, but it was only with the aid of the torch on my phone
that I was able to detect the barely visible join where the timber floor-
boards had been skilfully cut. I looked up at the others.

'It's a trapdoor. Do any of you have a knife?'

Sergeant Gallo reached into his pocket and produced a Swiss army
knife. With the aid of this, he managed to prise the trapdoor sufficiently so
we could get our fingers underneath it and lift. We found ourselves looking
into a dark pit. Oscar had his nose pointing unerringly downwards and I
caught hold of his collar in case he might decide to jump into the abyss.
The torch on my phone showed the rough-hewn walls, a couple of metres

deep, and I caught my breath as I saw a familiar figure lying face down and motionless in the dirt, her left arm splayed out at an unnatural angle. I felt as if a cold knife had been driven into my chest, and I immediately realised what the ladder was for. With the aid of the sergeant, I lowered it into the hole until it touched the bottom. He reached for the top step, but I stopped him.

'Let me go first. It's my partner, Anna. I need to go to her. Would you hold onto Oscar for me?'

To an accompaniment of plaintive whining from Oscar, I climbed down the ladder until my foot touched the ground. I pulled out the torch again as I fell to my knees and reached forward towards Anna. Acting on instinct born of long experience while my brain swirled with the implications of what I was seeing, I laid my hand against the carotid artery in her neck. The wave of relief that surged through me as I felt a distinct pulse was almost overpowering, and I suddenly felt tears in my eyes. She was alive.

Wiping the back of my hand across my eyes, I cleared my throat and shouted up to the others. 'She's unconscious, but she's alive. Call the emergency services now. We'll need an ambulance and the fire brigade to haul her out of here.'

I turned back to Anna and did my best to cradle her head, desperately trying not to let my mind spin off into wild conjecture about how seriously injured she might be. For now, I told myself, all that counted was that she was still alive, but without Oscar's help, she could well have died.

I felt a burning anger rising up inside me. The investigation had suddenly got very personal.

19

WEDNESDAY

I spent the rest of the morning at the hospital. It would have been good to have had Oscar alongside me, but he wouldn't have been let in, so I had left him with Virgilio and Lina – giving them instructions to see that he got the biggest steak available. The more I thought about it, I had absolutely no doubt that without his intervention, Anna might well be dead. Upon arrival at the hospital, they had wheeled her away to investigate the extent of her injuries and I'd been told to stay in the waiting room. The paramedics in the ambulance had quickly worked out that she had dislocated her left arm and that she had taken a blow to the forehead, rendering her unconscious.

Midway through the morning, a doctor came out to reassure me that she had regained consciousness and was doing well, and around half-past twelve, a nurse emerged to tell me that she was being moved to a private room. Shortly afterwards, I was finally allowed to see her. The nurse who accompanied me to the room told me I could have only a couple of minutes with her but repeated what the doctor had said. Anna was going to be fine.

These words were still echoing in my head as I tiptoed into the room. I was greeted by the sight of a battered Anna, lying back against a pile of pillows. Her left arm was in a sling, she had a spectacular black eye, there were surgical dressings on her cheek and a bigger dressing across her fore-head. Her eyes opened as she heard the door and a little smile appeared on her face as she saw me, although she looked as if she had just gone ten rounds in the ring with Tyson Fury. I hurried over to her bedside and, once again, felt tears stinging the corners of my eyes. I stood there and looked down at her, for once, totally lost for words. She reached out her good arm and caught hold of my hand.

'It's all right, *carissimo*, I'm all right, really. The doctor told me I have a hard head.'

I took her hand in both of mine and did my best to avoid blubbing like a baby as I finally managed to string a handful of words together. 'The doctor says you're going to be all right. Thank God.'

'How did you find me?' Her expression became more serious. 'I've been lying here trying to remember, but it's all so vague. Oscar and I were in the overgrown field, and I saw that the doors of the shed were open. I presume I must have walked over there but I can't remember anything else until I woke up here in the hospital.'

I pulled up a chair and sat down beside her while I gave her a very quick summary of how we had managed to track her down. The smile returned to her face.

'Oscar really is a very special dog, isn't he?'

I didn't bother answering. We both knew the answer to that one. 'The nurse said I can only stay for a couple of minutes. You have to sleep now. Do you have any idea who might have done this to you?'

I saw her shake her head and then wince. 'Like I said, the last thing I can remember is seeing the shed with the doors open. It could have been anybody.' She gave my hand a little squeeze. 'Don't worry, Dan, I'm all right and I'm going to get better, properly better. They say they're just keeping me here for a while to be sure there are no after-effects of the blow to the head.' The smile returned to her lips. 'You look terrible. Go off now and let me sleep. And grab yourself a cold beer and some food; you look as if you could use it. Oh yes, and make sure you give Oscar a hug from me, a really big hug.'

I kissed her and left her to rest. The nurse told me I could come back at the end of the afternoon and I wandered out of the hospital feeling drained. In the space of a few hours, I had experienced emotional highs and lows that had left me weary but, ultimately, heartened. If I had been harbouring any doubts about my relationship with Anna – and I hadn't – the events of this morning had underscored the great affection I felt for her. Coming so close to losing her had finally managed to break through my ridiculous English reserve and made me realise how bleak life without her would be. I loved her dearly.

Cheered by this realisation, I headed down the hill until I reached the waterside and strolled along a stretch of quay where a swanky cruise ship with no fewer than nine decks was disgorging a seemingly never-ending stream of tourists. I hastily headed in the opposite direction until I found a suitably quiet backstreet bar where I obeyed the order Anna had given me. As I savoured a big glass of cold beer, I gradually relaxed and let my mind move on to exactly what we had discovered today – apart from Anna's battered body.

Aldo Graziani's shed had obviously been erected so as to conceal the entrance to the hole in the ground. What this was remained to be seen, but it might have been an ancient mine. It was very fortunate that this had been only a couple of metres deep or Anna wouldn't have stood a chance. While waiting for the ambulance and the fire brigade, I had been able to make out a series of niches cut in the mine walls, and in the shadowy entrance to one of these, I had at first thought I'd spotted another person, standing silently watching me. I had been on the point of calling down one of the armed police officers when I had realised that what I was looking at was a statue. When the emergency services had arrived and set about the delicate task of strapping Anna to a stretcher and winching her up the mineshaft, I had investigated my surroundings more closely.

The first discovery I had made had been that behind this finely carved statue of a severe-looking man in a long robe with a remarkably modern hairstyle, there were no fewer than three other statues of varying sizes. It was clear that I had found a repository of ancient antiquities, no doubt worth millions of euros. Had they been stored here centuries ago or had they been unearthed elsewhere and then hidden here for safekeeping more recently? No doubt the experts would be able to establish this, but what was clear was that these statues had to be the source of Aldo Graziani's newfound wealth.

The next question was who else had known about this stockpile? Of course, at least one person must have – and that was whoever had assaulted Anna. She had told me that she'd seen the doors of the shed wide open, while we had had to smash our way in. This indicated that her assailant had had a key. A thought occurred to me and I called Virgilio, who told me he'd been working closely with Piero Fontana all morning. After giving him the good news that Anna was conscious, compos mentis and making good progress, I asked him a question. 'Have you any idea whether the police have been able to find the key to the shed?'

'No, Piero says his people have searched the reception area at the camp-site and they're going back over every inch of Aldo's villa, but so far without success.'

'And there were no keys found in his pockets when the body was taken to the morgue?'

'In his pocket there was a wallet, a phone, some coins and a ring holding the key to his villa and his car, but there was no trace of keys to any of the campsite buildings or to the shed.'

'And that's highly suspicious. At the very least, I would have expected him to be carrying keys to the campsite and I'm sure that he would have carried the shed key with him at all times, so I reckon the murderer took them after assaulting him. On that basis, it seems likely that the person who so nearly killed Anna also killed Aldo. Agreed?'

'That's the conclusion we've come to as well. Now we've got to work out who that might be. Piero's instigated a search of the chalet where Teresa Franceschini lives as well as the home of Fabio Morso. Piero's also been questioning the Japanese man and the shopkeepers from Lucca. His people have been searching their rooms as well and I'm waiting to hear from him if they've discovered anything. What about you? Where are you? You travelled over to Portoferraio in the ambulance, didn't you? Can I come and give you a lift home?'

I protested that I could easily take a taxi but he insisted, and twenty-five minutes later, he arrived to pick me up. Sitting on the back seat of his car, looking like visiting royalty, was none other than Oscar, and when he saw me, he leapt forward onto the front seat, tail wagging furiously, and he was halfway out of the passenger window before I managed to stop him. I made a real fuss of him and then persuaded him to return to the back seat while I sat down alongside Virgilio with a cold canine nose breathing in my ear.

'*Ciao*, Virgilio, thanks for picking me up.' I produced a smile. 'You do know it's an offence to have a dog unsecured on the back seat of a vehicle, don't you?'

He grinned at me. 'I had no option. There was no way Oscar was going to let me come and pick you up on my own. Besides, he's been very well behaved. Now, tell me all about Anna.'

As he threaded his way through the busy traffic of the town, I told him everything I had been told at the hospital and added that, in spite of her dislocated arm and her head wounds, she had been very lucky.

I saw his face grow more serious. 'She was *extremely* lucky. Whoever pushed her into that hole in the ground must have known that she could easily have been killed. By the way, Forensics say that the wound to her forehead was caused when her head struck the feet of one of the stone statues.'

I shivered yet again. 'And as far as I'm concerned, the finger of suspicion surely points at either Teresa Franceschini or Fabio Morso. Have Piero's people found anything in their accommodation – come to think of it, where does Fabio Morso live?'

'He's staying at his father's old place, about a kilometre down the road from the campsite. There's a team going through it as we speak.' He glanced across at me as we headed along the remarkably narrow 'main' road towards Porto Azzurro, lined with umbrella pines and occasional farmsteads. Compared to the coast, the hinterland of the island was remarkably undeveloped. 'You look terrible, fancy a drink?'

'That's what Anna said – the looking terrible thing and the drink thing. I've just had a beer, but I really need to eat something now. I feel empty.' At my use of the word 'eat,' I heard movement at my ear and a wave of malodorous dog breath blew past me. 'Did Oscar get his steak?'

'Not yet. The kitchen staff were crazy busy, but we can remedy that right now.' With that, he pulled off the road into the car park of a little restaurant bearing the auspicious name of The Grill – written in English.

All around us were fields and hills, and the restaurant itself looked more like a decrepit barn than a glitzy McDonald's. On the far side of the building, protected from the gusty wind, there was a line of tables sheltered beneath an even more decrepit-looking pergola whose timbers bowed alarmingly under the weight of a mass of vines. It was almost two o'clock and most of the other diners were already on their desserts or coffees by now, but a waiter assured us that we were still in time to eat. He showed us to a table at the far end of the terrace and provided us with a verbal menu. It didn't take long. As far as I could tell, it was a choice of meat, meat or meat – all of it grilled.

We opted to split a mixed grill accompanied by roast potatoes and a fresh artichoke salad. The waiter disappeared for less than a minute before returning with a carafe of anonymous red wine, another of water, and a basket containing bread and grissini. With the aid of a glass of the remarkably drinkable wine and a couple of breadsticks shared with Oscar, I was soon feeling more like my old self again after what had been a traumatic morning. Virgilio chatted about all sorts, ranging from the beauty of the island to the quality of the wine, and I could tell that he was deliberately steering clear of the subject of the two murders and the assault on Anna. It was good of him, but, now that I was feeling more normal again, I brought up the subject myself.

'If we assume for the moment that Aldo's death is somehow connected with the illegal antiquities trade, that still doesn't help us work out whether we're looking for one murderer or two. What do you think?'

At that moment, the waiter returned with a huge wooden platter loaded with meat, accompanied by a pile of little roast potatoes. Alongside this was a dish of fresh raw artichoke hearts in an olive oil and lemon-juice dressing. A heavy, black head landed on my thigh as Oscar's nose strained upwards towards what was a most appealing aroma. I glanced across at Virgilio and grinned.

'I'm very glad I resisted the temptation to order a separate steak for Oscar. There's enough meat here to feed half a dozen people.'

And there was. There were no fewer than four grilled kebabs packed with pieces of steak interspersed with chunks of red pepper, courgette and aubergine, a grilled chicken breast that looked as if it had come from a massive beast the size of an ostrich, a dozen ribs and a curled-up, spiral Tuscan sausage the size of a side plate. The mountain of roast potatoes alone would have fed a large family, and the artichoke salad looked most inviting.

We helped ourselves to the food and to the delight of my four-legged friend, I dismembered one of the kebabs and handed him down a series of succulent pieces of steak, followed by a chunk of the chicken breast that was the size of a pack of cards. There was disbelief in his eyes as the tasty titbits kept on coming but, although I'm normally against feeding him from the table, he deserved every single bit of the feast. It's not every day your dog saves your partner's life. As Anna said, he's a very special dog.

We didn't do a lot of talking for about a quarter of an hour, and it was only when our appetites – not Oscar's, of course – began to wane that the conversation picked up again and Virgilio provided the answer to my original question.

'I've been thinking about this case a lot and I'm coming around to the conclusion that the object of the killer's intentions has to have been Aldo rather than Ignazio. I reckon the first death was a mistake, although Ignazio's background made us immediately assume that he'd been deliberately murdered. I think we're looking at a single killer and my money's on the woman, Teresa Franceschini, either out of greed or frustrated affection. Is that what you think?'

I swallowed a final piece of kebab and washed it down with a mouthful of wine before replying. 'You could well be right. There's definitely something hard and calculating about her, although I still can't pin down a viable motive for murder, unless it's to get her hands on the Etruscan artefacts. I must confess that I'm not totally giving up on the idea of two different killers, but it's definitely looking more likely the work of one person. I wonder how Piero Fontana got on with his interviews.'

At that moment, Virgilio's phone started ringing and I was immediately on full alert when I heard him greet the caller. '*Ciao*, Piero, anything new?'

The inspector spoke to Virgilio for almost five minutes and all I could hear were occasional grunts or one-word comments from Virgilio before the call ended and he dropped his phone back onto the table.

'Several interesting developments. The Japanese police have been amazingly efficient and have already replied to the query about Tatsuo Tanaka. The bad news from our point of view is that although the mother of Laura Bracco, Ignazio Graziani's second victim, was born in Nagoya, she and her family moved back to Tokyo when she was only three months old. The father was a serving army officer and he was subsequently transferred to the Japanese embassy in Rome as Defence Attaché when the girl was only five and she grew up in Italy. Tanaka has lived all his life in Nagoya and he gets a clean bill of health – his father's a judge, no less – so it looks like that's a dead end.'

'You said *several* interesting developments. What else did he say? Any joy with the couple from Lucca and their antique shop?'

'Much more promising. When Piero's people searched their room at the hotel, they found nothing, but when they opened the boot of the car, they found a box containing two bronze statuettes wrapped in tissue paper. Signor Giardino was unable to provide an invoice for these items and was very evasive about how he'd come by them. Photos of them were sent to the National Archaeological Museum in Naples and they have been positively identified as of Etruscan origin and the couple have been arrested. They're at the station right now being interviewed, and the TPC have been notified and are sending two officers. No prizes for guessing who they'll be.'

'That's very interesting. Could it be that Giardino and his wife are the elusive Tuscan handlers? If so, it should be possible to get them to identify the source not only of these two bronze statuettes but also of the larger, more valuable objects that have emerged from the island. I'm not a betting man, but I would happily stake a hundred euros on Aldo Graziani's name popping up.'

Virgilio took a final piece of meat from his plate, handed the remaining piece of sausage to Oscar and set his fork back down. 'That's enough for me. No more meat for a week – no, make that a month. And, yes, I'm also quietly confident that Giardino will supply the missing link to Aldo.' He took a sip of wine. 'But I fail to see what interest they could have had in murdering him. Surely if Aldo was regularly producing high-value arte-facts, it was in their interests to keep him sweet and alive.'

'I suppose they might have decided to do away with him and try to take over his operation for themselves.'

Virgilio's phone started ringing again. This time, it was a relatively short call and there was a broad smile on his face when it finished. 'That was Piero again. Forensics have found a toothbrush at Aldo's villa. DNA testing proves that it's been used by Teresa Franceschini. Maybe it was a crime of passion after all. She's being taken to the station as we speak.' He picked up his glass and clinked it against mine. 'Cheers, Dan, I think we might be nearing a conclusion.'

20

WEDNESDAY LATE AFTERNOON

I drove back over to see Anna at five. I parked in the shade and left Oscar in the van with the windows open while I went into the hospital. To my delight, she was sitting up in bed, eating what looked like crème caramel. There was even a bit more colour in her cheeks and my spirits soared. My instincts were to go across to the bed and hug her tightly, but her damaged arm and surgical dressings to her head and face restricted me to just sitting down beside her and catching hold of her good hand in both of mine.

'*Ciao, carissima*, you're looking better.'

She smiled. 'And so are you. Did you take my advice and have something to eat and drink?'

Now it was my turn to smile. 'Yes, very definitely – and Oscar got a bellyful of meat. Have the doctors said anything about when you can come home?'

'They want to keep me in overnight to be sure that there are no after-effects but, hopefully, some time tomorrow morning, I should be discharged. I'll need to keep my left arm in a sling for a few days, but they tell me I should be able to use it normally again in less than a week. How's the investigation going?'

I gave her a quick summary of the latest developments and she looked mildly surprised. 'So do you think it was Teresa who pushed me down that mine? I wouldn't have thought she would have had the strength.'

To be honest, I'd been harbouring the same doubts, but I just gave her a few platitudes about the police knowing best and left it at that for now. It then emerged that she had been starting to get a bit more clarity about the events of this morning. She told me she could remember being in the field, seeing the doors of the shed open and going across to take a look inside. Although she had no recollection of the blow to the head or her fall, she did come up with a fascinating snippet of information.

'It may mean nothing, but I'm sure there was a flash of yellow, bright yellow, as I peered in through the doors. I've no idea what it was – it certainly wasn't the sun – but I'm quite sure about it. It's just about the last memory I have.'

I found myself leaning forward towards her. 'You're saying you saw something yellow. What sort of something?'

She snorted with frustration. 'I just can't remember. If I had to guess, I would say it was probably clothing, but I may be completely wrong. Hopefully, as my brain begins to clear and the memories start coming back, I might have a better idea.'

This was potentially very interesting, and I knew I needed to make an urgent call to the inspector. He was currently interviewing Teresa Franceschini and when I had seen her first thing this morning, she had been wearing a bright-yellow top. Was this the proof we needed that she had callously pushed Anna into the mine and left her to die?

I was allowed only ten minutes with Anna this time, so I sat with her and we chatted about all sorts, including the debt of gratitude she owed to Oscar and the meaty reward he had already received. Finally, at exactly five-fifteen, a nurse appeared at the door and indicated that my time was up. I gave Anna a gentle kiss and left the room.

As soon as I got outside, I headed for the van and opened the back door. Oscar looked out hopefully, but I had something to do before I could take him for a walk. I called Piero Fontana.

'*Ciao*, Piero. Sorry to disturb you, but I've just come from the hospital and Anna's remembered something.'

'Excellent. The doctors told us we couldn't interview her until tomorrow. Anything significant?'

I related what Anna had said about the colour yellow and he gave a satisfied grunt. 'I still have Teresa Franceschini here and I'm about to have another go at her. I'm gradually making progress and she's finally admitted that she and Aldo were having an affair, although she just referred to it as an "arrangement". Talk about cold-blooded! It's patently clear that she was granting him sexual favours in the hope of getting him either to marry her or give her a share of the business. When I say "business", I'm still trying to decide whether that's just the campsite or whether she and Aldo were in on the antiquities racket together. It won't surprise you to hear that she disclaims any knowledge of it. This information about the yellow garment could potentially be a game changer.'

I thought I'd better sound a note of caution. 'Anna couldn't swear that it was a garment. She just said she saw something bright yellow.'

'Let's see what Teresa Franceschini has to say to this. I'll catch up with you and Virgilio later.'

I slipped my phone back into my pocket and sat on the tailgate for a few moments, wondering if Teresa would turn out to be the killer – and whether this was just Aldo's murderer or the person responsible for both deaths. The fact that she had finally admitted lying about her relationship with Aldo was significant and showed what a convincing liar she could be. She had been quite adamant in her denials before, so maybe her claim of not having any involvement in the murders would also prove to be false.

I was still lost in my thoughts when Oscar's hairy head landed on my lap and he looked up at me in supplication. I could take a hint.

'Right, dog, let's go and have a good long walk. Does that appeal?'

It did.

I drove back to the hotel and, on impulse, decided to go back up to the overgrown field to see if the police had been able to uncover any more clues. The wind felt as if it was beginning to subside and as I crossed the windsurfing beach, Ingrid gave me a wave and mouthed the word, 'Tomorrow'. I eyed the waves apprehensively and hoped they would have calmed down again by the morning.

By now, the track up through the field was exhibiting the marks of the

series of vehicles that had used it today, ranging from the fire-brigade jeep
to the ambulance and several police cars, although all of them had long
since left. Police tape had been strung around the shed, the doors we had
broken had been mended and secured by a hefty padlock attached to a
solid, metal hasp, and a large, blue notice on one of the doors indicated
clearly that this was a crime scene and access was forbidden. There were
no police officers to be seen, so I couldn't ask what progress they might
have made and, in consequence, Oscar and I set off again up the hill until
we reached another good observation point three or four hundred metres
further up. In spite of the cooling breeze, we were both hot by now so we
turned off the track and struggled through the vines towards a stunted,
very thorny tree, where we could sit in the shade and rest.

Back down the hill from here, the view was stunning. The rocky coast-
line of the island surrounded by the deep azure sea with the white water of
the waves was like something out of a tourist brochure and even the overgrown field itself added a splash of colour to the dusty hillside. It was
immediately clear that the shed had been placed in an auspicious position.
The hillside definitely flattened out a bit down there and I could just make
out the darker earth of the spring I had spotted the previous day. To my
amateur eye, it definitely struck me as a very sensible place for the forefa-
thers of Elba's present-day inhabitants to have built a settlement. Maybe
Stefano would be able to locate his long-lost mining community this
winter when the greenery died back. Had there even been a temple or
some such here, which would have accounted for the statues? I hoped he
would find it. Even if I hadn't yet solved the Graziani murder case, maybe
I'd come up with something that might help his historical investigations.

I was about to leave the welcome shade of the little tree and start
heading back downhill again when I heard a crunching noise behind me. I
turned my head to see Fabio Morso, once again in full cycling gear, go
shooting down the rough track on his mountain bike.

His bright-yellow mountain bike.

He was travelling at pace and concentrating on negotiating the rough
track so he didn't see Oscar and me. I stayed in the shade of the tree and
looked on as he bumped his way downhill until he was level with the shed.
At this point, he braked hard, skidding almost to a halt, before turning left

and heading straight for it. I saw him dismount and disappear around the back of the shed with the bike. To my surprise, he didn't reappear. I waited for about five minutes but there was no sign of him so, finally, I got up and started making my way down the track again.

When I came to the turn-off for the shed, I pulled out my phone and called Piero Fontana, but there was no reply, so I called Virgilio. Keeping my voice low, I told him what I'd just seen and asked him if he could get a message to the inspector. I told him that this could just be idle curiosity on the part of Fabio Morso, but I had a feeling there might be more to it than that. Certainly, the flashy, yellow bike had stirred up a whole lot of suspicious thoughts in my head. Virgilio sounded equally fascinated and told me he would make sure a message got through to the police and then he would come and join me.

I waited for another five minutes but saw no sign of Morso. It was as if he had just disappeared into thin air. A noise attracted my attention and I saw Virgilio sprinting up the track towards me. He was red in the face and sweating profusely, but I was impressed. For a man of fifty, he was a whole lot fitter than most senior police officers I'd met. He was panting when he got to me, but he still managed to speak.

'Where is he now? I spoke to Sergeant Gallo and he's on his way, but it'll be fifteen minutes before they get here from Portoferraio.'

I repeated what I'd seen and we exchanged glances while deciding what to do. He said it first. 'Well, there are two of us and only one of him – three if you include Oscar. I think we should go and take a look at what he's doing.'

I nodded in agreement. 'You take the right side, I'll take the left side, and I'll see you around the back of the shed. Okay?'

I kept hold of Oscar's collar while we approached the shed. Slowly, and as silently as possible, I made my way along the side, scanning the nearby vines for any sign of Morso or his bike, until I reached the back and cautiously risked a surreptitious glance around the corner. To my amazement, there was nobody there, nothing to be seen. Morso and his bike had disappeared without trace. Virgilio's face appeared around the other corner and we both shrugged our shoulders helplessly. Behind the shed was an impenetrable bank of vines, brambles and thorn bushes, and a pair of umbrella pines made it cool and dark back here. There was no way Morso could have disappeared into the undergrowth so that only left us with the shed itself. This was made of a series of wooden panels, bolted onto a modern-looking, metal frame, but there was no sign of a doorway. I had almost given up on any chance of finding a back door when I noticed Oscar with his nose to the ground.

Although he has definitely inherited the retriever gene, he's never displayed any great talents as a sniffer dog – unless it's food or other dogs' backsides – but there was clearly something here that interested him. I crouched down and took a closer look at the earth by the back wall and suddenly noticed something. On the hard, dry ground, I could just about make out the impressions made by the chunky tyres of a mountain bike. What was strange was that after running parallel to the rear of the shed for several feet, they suddenly turned in a right angle and stopped right up against the back wall. I let my hand run over the timber surface until I felt the faintest cut in the wood. I pulled out my phone and, with the aid of the torch, I realised that what I was touching was a beautifully concealed door-way. There was a rear entrance to the shed after all.

I looked up at Virgilio and held a finger to my lips while pointing out what I had found. I saw realisation dawn on his face so, slowly and quietly, we tiptoed away until we could whisper to each other without fear of being overheard. He glanced at his watch before speaking.

'Gallo and his team should be here in ten minutes or so. What do you think? Shall we try and go in or do we just wait until the police get here?'

'I think it's pretty clear that he's in there now, so if one of us guards the front gates – even if they are securely bolted – and the other stays here guarding the back, we should have him pretty well hemmed in. If you take the front, you can fill the police in when they arrive. If he tries to make his exit that way before they get here, just shout and I'll come running. And the same applies for me if he tries to make a run for it through the back door. All right?'

He nodded and tiptoed off, leaving Oscar and me to police the rear of the shed. I positioned myself at one corner so that I could keep an eye on both the back and side walls and settled down to wait while Oscar sprawled in the shade alongside me. While I stood there, I did my best to make sense of the situation so far. It was clear that Morso knew his way around this building intimately and I wondered what had brought him here now. He must have known from the police tape surrounding the shed, if not from the local bush telegraph, that the police had been here. Had he come to check whether the pit with its hidden treasure trove had been found? Whatever the reason, one thing was clear: if he knew about the hidden door, then he must surely have known about the concealed trap-door in the floor giving access to the statues. In consequence, there was every likelihood that he had been the person who had assaulted Anna and left her for dead. I felt another wave of anger welling up inside me and I did my best to suppress it. This wasn't the moment for thought of retaliation, it was a time for a cool head.

I was still standing there thinking hard a few minutes later when I started to hear distant sirens as what sounded like a pair of police cars came charging along the road and turned up the track towards us. The sound must have filtered through to the inside of the shed because I suddenly saw the hidden door swing open as the figure of Fabio Morso emerged with his bike. He already had his foot on one pedal when I threw myself at him, knocking him and his bike to the ground while I ended up on top of him. I shouted at the top of my voice and a few seconds later, Virgilio arrived and, between us, we pinned the man down while Oscar stood by and watched the antics of the three humans rolling around in the dirt with an expression of puzzled amusement on his hairy face.

21

WEDNESDAY EVENING

Sergeant Gallo didn't waste any time. He clapped handcuffs onto Fabio Morso's wrists and instructed two officers to take him straight back to the inspector for interrogation. Morso himself didn't say a word to me or to anybody else as he was marched off, but the expression on his face spoke volumes. The patina of bonhomie that he had demonstrated when we'd questioned him at the hotel had been replaced by a sullen acceptance of his fate. He had been caught out, and now he knew he would have to face the consequences.

There was another surprise in store for us when we looked in through the cleverly concealed rear doorway. I peered into the gloom, expecting to see the inside of the empty shed, but found myself looking at a blank piece of timber only a few feet in front of me. It took me a moment before I realised that in fact, the hidden door led into a long, narrow corridor occupying the full width of the shed. The shed had been constructed with a false rear wall so as to create a hidden storeroom. Inside this storeroom, there was a stunning stone statue half as tall as I was of what looked like a Greek god. On a shelf alongside it, there were five beautiful black and orange bowls and a finely moulded terracotta head of a young boy with a curly fringe. I had no idea what the possible value of these pieces might be, but I had little doubt that I was looking at a treasure trove worth millions.

It was now clear why Morso had risked coming here. Somehow, he must have learned of Aldo's cache of Etruscan treasures and had come to check that at least some of them had not yet been discovered by the police. I wished I'd thought to search his pockets before they took him away. The more I thought about it, the more I suspected that he had been the person that Anna had run into earlier. The yellow bike was probably what had stuck in her memory, and the fact that she had seen the shed doors open told me that he had come armed with a key, and almost certainly that key had come from Aldo Graziani's pocket. As well as the attempted murder of Anna, it was looking ever more likely that Morso would also be facing the charge of murdering Aldo.

Virgilio and I stood discussing what had just happened and the chain of events began to crystallise in our minds. Presumably, five years ago, Aldo Graziani had learned of precious artefacts being unearthed and sold on the black market by Fabio Morso's father, Ernesto. Blackmailing him with the threat of reporting him to the police, Aldo had been able to buy this land at a fraction of its real price and then erect this cleverly built shed over the top of the pit so he could operate with impunity. Old Ernesto Morso had died two months ago, and presumably, his son had decided to take revenge on the man he saw as responsible for his father's decline and death. Maybe his father had left a letter or had revealed all to his son on his deathbed, and Fabio had hoped to help himself to a fortune in antiquities in the process.

Virgilio and I agreed that this seemed the most likely explanation, and hopefully, Anna's memory would keep on coming back and she would soon be able to give a positive identification of at least the bike, if not her assailant. Catching Morso red-handed among the Etruscan treasures here provided proof that he had known about the artefacts and this linked him to Aldo's death. Hopefully, the police would find the key to the shed in his possession – ideally with Aldo's DNA on it – and this would provide yet another valuable piece of evidence to support the assertion that Fabio Morso had been responsible for his murder. The fact was, however, that unless he confessed, I questioned whether there was enough evidence for him to be sent for trial with a realistic prospect of a guilty verdict.

Either way, this still left us with the same unanswered question: what about Ignazio? Had Morso killed him by mistake, or had somebody completely different murdered him? Alternatively, had it been suicide, or had his death been an accident as Inspector Bellini had believed all along? I still had a feeling in my gut that Ignazio's death had been murder, but, unless Morso held up his hand and admitted to it, it was looking increasingly as if the trail had gone cold. I glanced across at Virgilio and shrugged my shoulders.

'Unless it was mistaken identity, I can see no reason why Morso should have killed Ignazio. It's very possible that Ignazio was killed by his brother, who had a lot to gain from his death, but there's no way we can prove that now. That leaves us with the couple from the antiques shop in Lucca. I suppose it's possible they might have intended to kill Aldo on Saturday night, but in the dark, they ended up killing his brother, but there seems no logical reason why they would have wanted to kill the goose that produced the golden eggs. As for Teresa Franceschini, it looks like she's in the clear if Morso killed Aldo. I can't see that she had any motive to kill Ignazio and surely she wouldn't have confused him for his brother. Tatsuo Tanaka has received a clean bill of health so I suppose we're going to have to accept that Ignazio was either murdered by his brother, or his death may well have been an accident after all.'

Virgilio nodded slowly and there was resignation in his voice when he responded. 'You're right, of course, Dan, maybe it was an accident. It's just that there's something deep down inside me that still believes he was murdered but, like you say, there's no hard evidence against anybody else, so I suppose I'm just going to have to let it go.'

I gave him a wry smile. 'I know how you feel, but at least it means you and Lina should be able to enjoy a few days of peaceful holiday now. The same applies to me. I'm going to have to look after Anna when she comes out of hospital, so I have a feeling she and I will both be having a very quiet few days as well.'

He produced a little grin. 'Don't tell me you're using Anna's injuries as an excuse for giving up on your windsurfing course? I'm sure she wouldn't want you to do that.'

To be honest, this was a bit too close to the truth, but I did my best to appear nonchalant. 'No, I enjoyed the windsurfing – well, after the baptism of fire of the first day – so if she wants me to carry on, I will.' I grinned back at him. 'Although, between you and me, you're right, and I'd be more than happy just to lie on the beach and try and forget everything that's happened.'

I glanced at my watch and was mildly surprised to see that it was only six-thirty. So much had happened since I'd seen Anna in hospital little more than an hour ago. I toyed with the idea of calling her to tell her about Fabio Morso but decided to leave her in peace for tonight. Hopefully, a good sleep would help her recovery. Once again, I found myself thinking about what had so nearly happened, and what a cataclysmic effect her death would have had on me. It was ironic that it had taken an attempt on her life for me to realise how much she meant to me and how empty my life would be without her.

The now familiar sight of the scene of crime team van bumping up the track told us that there was nothing more for us here, so we bade farewell to Sergeant Gallo and headed back in the direction of the hotel. As we walked through the campsite and past the pointing finger marked Reception, I wondered whether Piero Fontana would now release Teresa, or whether he intended to keep her in custody. As far as I could see, unless she had admitted to murdering Ignazio – and I was still at a loss to see why she should have done that – or been involved with the illicit antiquities trade, he had nothing on her. Maybe the events of the last few days would even work in her favour and she might find herself promoted to manager of the whole Graziani empire.

Virgilio went off to look for Lina while I went out onto the terrace and slumped down at our table. Oscar followed suit at my feet with a heartfelt sigh. I knew how he felt. It had been an eventful day and I felt pretty weary – although I had to confess that the huge lunch might have contributed – so when the waitress came out, I ordered a freshly pressed lemonade rather than anything alcoholic. It was still early and none of the other guests had appeared, so I sat back and did my best to relax. It was still light enough to see across the water to the mainland of Tuscany and I found myself wondering if an Etruscan miner had once sat in this very same spot and relaxed after a hard day in the iron mine. Presumably, somebody had chosen the old shaft as a perfect spot in which to hide the precious statues, although mystery still surrounded their origin. Maybe there really had once been a settlement or even a temple up there, and Stefano would be able to find its remains and enhance his thesis.

My mind then inevitably went back to the writer's block that had been plaguing me for weeks and I found myself analysing the way this case appeared to be resolving itself, in the hope that something here might help me with the problem I faced in my work of fiction. Now that Morso had been arrested, I played with the revenge scenario in my head as I sipped my lemonade. But revenge for what? Had the dead man in San Gimignano cheated somebody as Aldo had done, or had it been an affair of the heart? Maybe if I introduced a love interest...?

As far as the first death here was concerned, there was always the possibility that Ignazio had deliberately thrown himself off the cliff, although I had serious doubts about that. What, I wondered, might have driven the character in my book to do the same? Desperation or guilt, but about what? And, of course, it was still feasible and maybe even probable that Ignazio had simply stumbled over the edge under the influence of an awful lot of alcohol. Maybe the Graziani case was going to be of no help to me and my writer's block at all.

I was still mulling all this over when my phone started ringing. I was delighted to see that it was Anna.

'*Ciao*, Anna, it's great to hear from you.' At my feet, I saw Oscar look up and wag his tail as he heard me say her name. 'Oscar sends his love – and so do I. How are you feeling?'

'I feel a whole lot better. The nurse brought me a plate of lasagne and I managed to eat most of it. It wasn't quite up to the standard of the Hotel Augustus, but it wasn't bad for hospital food.' She sounded more animated and I felt an overwhelming feeling of relief. 'Anyway, the reason I'm calling is to tell you that I've gradually been remembering more about what happened. That yellow thing I saw at the shed, it was a bike, one of those chunky mountain bikes. I'm sure of it. It was leaning against the inside of the doorframe. Does that help?'

'That helps enormously.' I went on to tell her what had happened since I had last seen her and how this snippet of information from her was likely to prove highly significant. We chatted some more and I told her I would come to the hospital at nine the next morning to see if she was going to be discharged. As soon as the call ended, I phoned the inspector and passed on what Anna had just told me.

He gave a satisfied grunt. 'That's excellent news. Morso has been stonewalling, but we checked the contents of his pockets and we found two sets of keys. One set matches his house and car, but the others are confirmed as belonging to Aldo Graziani and one of them is a long, flat security key. We've checked and, yes, it's the key to the shed. Morso's prints are all over the inside of the shed and, in particular, on the trapdoor in the floor leading to the pit with the statues. I think we've got him.'

'For the attempted murder of Anna and trafficking, yes, but what about Aldo's murder? Any evidence to link him to that, apart from the keys?'

'The keys are pretty damning. There's no way Aldo would have handed over the keys to his villa and the campsite along with the key to the shed unless he was pressured. A German couple at the campsite claim to have seen somebody of Morso's description with Aldo just before midnight on Monday. The two men were walking by the shore. We're organising an identity parade, and hopefully, that will be the final bit of proof we need.'

'That sounds excellent. What about Teresa or the Giardino couple?'

'That's the other bit of good news. Once it sank in that we suspected the Giardino couple of being Aldo's murderers, they caved in and admitted being the local handlers for Etruscan antiquities, although they vehemently deny any involvement in either death. They've told us that Aldo was indeed their contact here and, most interesting of all, they said that they took a phone call at lunchtime today from none other than Fabio Morso, keen to pick up the business that his father started. We've checked the phones and it's as they say. I don't think they're murderers, but we've passed them on to the TPC, and they are going to be in big trouble with the *Carabinieri*.'

'And Teresa? Any involvement in either of the murders or in the antiquities racket?'

'No to both, I think. I've given her a rocket for lying to us about her relationship with Aldo and I've told her I could still charge her with obstructing a murder investigation, but I've released her and I see no point in having anything more to do with her. It's clear to me that she made a cynical decision to initiate a relationship with Aldo in the hope of getting her hands on his money. She's a tough character, but I don't see her as a murderer and we have nothing else on her.'

'And Ignazio's death?'

'Given that we have a complete absence of any kind of evidence against anybody, including Fabio Morso, it's looking more and more likely that Bellini was right. The man was hopelessly drunk and he fell off the clifftop all by himself. I'll give it until tomorrow and then, unless anything else turns up, I'll leave it as misadventure.'

When the call ended, I sat there holding the phone, reflecting on what Fontana had said. With no proof to the contrary, it looked as though the death of Ignazio Graziani would remain a mystery. It was frustrating but there was little I could do about it. I glanced down at Oscar, who was stretched out on the floor, eyes closed.

'I'm afraid we'll never know, Oscar.'

He didn't even bother opening his eyes.

22

THURSDAY MORNING

When I got to the hospital at nine the next morning, it was to find that the doctors were still doing their rounds and I was instructed to come back in an hour. A friendly nurse gave me an encouraging smile and told me that Anna had had a good night and had been looking and sounding perky this morning. Hopefully, she would be returned to me before long.

It was still early enough for me to be able to find a parking space not far from the ferry port, and I took Oscar for a walk around the narrow streets of Portoferraio's *centro storico*, where I did some shopping in the shadow of the imposing Medici fortress perched malevolently above the harbour. The wind had dropped almost completely and the temperature was climbing fast, so Oscar and I hugged the shade as far as possible. After checking out a few shops and taking in the sights of the old town, we finally emerged from the narrow streets onto the waterfront. I found myself a table outside a café close to the bay and sat down to enjoy a cappuccino and the chance to catch my breath after what had been a fraught few days.

In front of me was a line of bushes and palm trees, beyond which was a narrow road and beyond that, the pedestrian promenade around the harbour. The water of the harbour itself was hardly visible through an unbroken line of yachts, moored stern first to the quay, and I wondered how much sailing the people on board these boats actually did. I wondered whether if they were to leave their precious parking spot – and it was just like a marine version of a crowded car park – another yacht would immediately sail up and occupy it. At least, I reflected, with windsurfing, you could just pick up your board and walk off with it.

Thought of windsurfing reminded me that I had another session to look forward to later today and I think it's fair to say my feelings on the subject were mixed. My right shoulder hurt from helping to break down the door to the shed, my left hip hurt where I had landed on the ground and wrestled with Fabio Morso and, after a broken night last night, I felt quite weary. Still, if Anna wanted me to do it, then I would obey her wishes.

My phone started ringing just as the waitress brought my coffee, and I waited until she'd left before answering.

'Ciao, Virgilio.' I hadn't seen him at breakfast, mainly because I'd had mine early so I could be sure of getting to the hospital in good time.

'Ciao, Dan, I've just been speaking to Piero and he told me that Fabio Morso has finally started talking. The German campers identified him in the ID parade as having been the last person seen with Aldo on Monday night. Faced with that evidence, he's admitted that he was with Aldo that night, but he's insisting that he had nothing to do with the murder.' His tone became more cynical. 'But he would say that, wouldn't he? His story is that he met up with Aldo and threatened him in exactly the same way that Aldo had threatened his father five years ago. As we thought, his father left a letter for him with his lawyer, and Fabio got it after the old man's death. Fabio faced Aldo with an ultimatum – either surrender the shed and its treasures to him or he would shop Aldo to the police.'

'And how did Aldo react?'

'As you can imagine. Morso says Aldo was furious, abusive and even threatening but finally, he agreed and handed over the key to the shed.'

'Along with all his other keys. That doesn't ring true. My money's on Morso killing Aldo and taking the keys. When he spoke to us the other day, he made it quite clear that he held Aldo responsible for his father's death, and I could well imagine him taking his revenge. Any sign of a murder weapon?'

'Forensics say it was a smooth, blunt instrument, and Piero's people are doing a sweep of the area as we speak, although finding that will be like finding a needle in a haystack.' He gave a frustrated hiss. 'Without that, Piero's stuck as far as a meaningful murder charge is concerned. He should be able to charge Morso with attempting to dispose of illegal antiquities but not murder at the moment. And, of course, there's Anna.'

I shared his frustration. 'At least Morso's assault on Anna is a pretty watertight case of attempted murder.'

'He admits that he was there, but he's been trying to say that that was an accident. He says when he saw a figure in the shed looking into the pit, he tried to grab her but she stumbled and fell in. It was only as she fell that he realised it was a woman and he intended going back later to let her out. He told Piero that when we caught up with him yesterday afternoon, he had gone there to do just that.'

I wasn't buying it. 'That sounds to me like a story he invented overnight in an attempt to avoid a charge of attempted murder. If he went to the shed to try and release her, what was he doing in the store at the far end? The trapdoor was in the main part of the shed.'

'That's exactly what Piero asked him, and he told me Morso says that because the front doors were padlocked, he was trying to get in that way. The fact is, though, that there's no communicating door from the store-room to the main part of the shed, so it's hard to see how he was going to do that apart from batter his way through.'

'I still believe he murdered Aldo in cold blood and if Oscar hadn't been on the case, he would have killed Anna as well.'

'My feelings entirely, but the public prosecutor might not be so sure. We just need to prove it.'

'And Ignazio? What does Morso say about *his* death?'

'He denies any involvement and it sounds as though he has a solid alibi for Saturday night.' I couldn't miss the frustration in Virgilio's voice. 'So as far as Ignazio's death is concerned, there's no evidence against anybody else, and Piero says he has no choice but to stick with Bellini's original decision. I suppose that's the sensible and pragmatic thing to do. Even if I still think it was murder, there's no evidence to prove that it wasn't simply a drunken accident.'

I sat there drinking my coffee and mulling over what Virgilio had said. Piero Fontana's decision not to investigate Ignazio's death any further was the logical course of action, but I still couldn't shift the sensation that we were missing a trick. The fact was, however, just as Virgilio and the inspector had said, without any evidence to the contrary, there was little anybody could do.

At ten o'clock, I was back at the hospital and I found Anna looking and sounding much more animated. She appeared positively delighted when I produced a bag of clothes I had picked up for her to replace what she had been wearing the day before. I helped her to get changed and, under the watchful eye of the nurse, she stood up and took her first hesitant steps, holding onto my arm with her good hand as she did so. Her other arm was in the sling and she was still sporting some impressive bandages, but she was out of bed and on the road to recovery, and I felt an overwhelming sense of relief. Although she kept hold of me, she was remarkably steady on her feet and she was able to give the nurse a hug and thank the doctor who came to see her off. Together, we walked to the lift and then out to the van, where Oscar gave her a rapturous welcome and Anna almost smothered him in a grateful embrace.

On the way back to the hotel, I told her I intended sticking to her like glue from now on, but she shook her head. 'I'll be fine, Dan. After a good strong coffee, I'm sure I'll be able to walk around to the windsurfing beach with you. You were making such good progress, you need to continue. I'll be sitting outside the café cheering you on.'

I smiled and agreed, although windsurfing wasn't high on my agenda at the moment. When we got back to the hotel, I led her to the terrace, where we found Lina and Virgilio, and they greeted her warmly. Anna ordered a double espresso and I did the same – I had a feeling I would need the energy for my windsurfing – and the drinks were brought out to us by Rita herself, who told us how appalled she had been to hear of Anna's 'accident'. Last night, Virgilio and I had deliberately avoided giving any details of what had happened in the pit until the inspector had been able to reach a satisfactory conclusion to the case. After distributing our coffees and giving Anna a sympathetic hug, Rita then revealed that she had brought an invitation.

'It's Signor Silvano's eightieth birthday today, and he's invited everybody to come for a glass of champagne in the lounge at seven.' She took a surreptitious look around, but the only other table was occupied by Tatsuo, his head buried in his phone. 'Any word on how the investigation's going? Is it true that the police have arrested someone?'

It sounded as though Rita was well informed, but Virgilio answered cautiously. 'It's possible that the inspector might have apprehended Aldo Graziani's killer, but I don't know any more than that at present. As far as Ignazio's death's concerned, he's dismissed it as misadventure. There's no evidence to the contrary.'

An expression of satisfaction appeared on her face. 'That's what I've always thought – he was so terribly drunk. Do you know who the inspector's arrested for Aldo's murder?'

Virgilio took refuge in obfuscation. 'No doubt we'll find out in due course, but all I know at the moment is that the inspector has a man in custody. If he turns out to be the perpetrator, that should mean that nobody here need have any more worries. If that is the case, that'll mean we'll all be free to go, but no doubt official word will be coming from the inspector in the course of the morning.'

'That's excellent news. I'll make sure I tell Signor Silvano. He's been most concerned about the effect of the investigation on the guests. Now he'll be able to celebrate his birthday in peace.'

As she went off to deliver the drinks invitation to Tatsuo, I reflected that today was already Thursday and my windsurfing course would be finishing tomorrow afternoon. I was a bit concerned that Ingrid had indicated that she intended making up the lessons missed due to the strong winds and I had a feeling today and tomorrow were going to be long days. Still, I told myself, I had told Anna I would go through with it, and I intended to keep my promise.

I was impressed to find that Anna was well able to walk across to the windsurfing beach, although I kept a precautionary hand on her good arm as we did so. When we got there – albeit later than we should have done – my fears were realised when Ingrid greeted us with the news that today's lunch break would be shortened to just half an hour, the afternoon session would go on until five-thirty, and tomorrow would be even longer. It was clear she intended making sure we got our money's worth. I smiled in response, but it was through gritted teeth. Stefano came over and it was immediately clear that they had both heard at least some of what had happened yesterday, and he and Ingrid were horrified to see Anna's wounds. She reassured them that the doctors had said that she would be fit and well again before too long.

Anna took a seat on the veranda outside the bar to watch my travails, while Oscar strategically positioned himself at her side – which just happened to be the side near the entrance through which people emerged in the course of the day bearing cakes, biscuits, ice creams and sandwiches. Anna told me later that all kinds of tasty morsels had ended up being offered to him when he had subjected the customers to his pathetic, *I'm fading away* look.

In fact, the day turned out to be very enjoyable. By lunchtime, I found I was managing to turn by tacking upwind seven or eight times out of ten without falling in, although gybing downwind remained fraught with problems, so I did my best to avoid trying that manoeuvre. As a result, when I came in for my abbreviated lunch break, I was able to count the number of times I had fallen in on the fingers of just two hands, and that was definite progress.

The progress continued after lunch and Tatsuo and I were finally encouraged to sail a bit further out to sea where the breeze was stronger and I thoroughly enjoyed zooming up and down. As I did so, I even had time to admire the view back towards the coast. From out here, I could see the beach, the campsite, the hotel, the overgrown field with the big shed and the imposing bulk of Monte Calamita stretching up behind it. It all looked remarkably peaceful now, but I shivered in spite of the heat as it occurred to me yet again just how close to death Anna had come. If it hadn't been for my four-legged friend, it was more than likely that she would be dead, and I knew that if that had happened, I would be bereft.

Finally, at well after five, Ingrid waved to me from the beach, indicating that it was time for me to head back to the shore.

The Greeks have a word for what happened next. I had no trouble in steering back towards the beach at pace, helped on by the little waves and feeling inordinately proud of myself. However, as I was approaching the shallows, I chose to do something very silly. I caught Anna's eye, raised my right hand from the boom and gave her a cheery wave. The sail, now only gripped by one hand, suddenly developed a mind of its own and two seconds later, I was propelled head first into the sea. To add insult to injury, the sail and mast landed on top of me and when I surfaced, I had to fight my way out from under the orange and blue fabric, coughing and spluttering.

Hubris, that's what the Greeks called it. 'Gross overconfidence leading to a tragic downfall,' as Anna gleefully explained to me when I joined her back at the bar. I thanked her for the Classics lesson and added the word to my vocabulary, making a mental note not to fall into that trap again.

I took a seat alongside her and we both ordered ice-cream sundaes complete with sprinkles and glacé cherries perched on top of mountains of whipped cream. Accompanied by half a litre of water, mine was delicious and I soon recovered from my moment of hubris. By the end of the ice cream, I was feeling weary but refreshed, and in fact, I was so refreshed that I told Anna I would give Oscar a quick walk before we headed back to get ready for Signor Silvano's birthday bash. Virgilio and Lina had joined Anna in the course of the afternoon and he accompanied Oscar and me as we walked up through the campsite, heading for the overgrown field where Oscar would be able to run about to his heart's content – although it was still very warm even as evening approached. When I spotted the pointing finger marked Reception, I glanced at Virgilio.

'Feel like having a word with Teresa Franceschini?'

He grinned. 'Definitely.'

We found Teresa in Reception, the radio now blaring out some unidentifiable Italian Europop song loud enough to set the teaspoon in her coffee cup jingling, and she treated us to a beaming smile. Mercifully, she reached for the volume control as we approached, and I began to hear myself think again. No doubt the ringing in my ears would subside with time.

'Hello, gentlemen. Isn't it a beautiful afternoon?'

Virgilio answered for both of us. 'It's a delightful afternoon, and it must be especially pleasant for you, now you're no longer being held at the police station. I imagine you're glad to be back.'

She didn't bat an eyelid. 'What is it you policemen say? I've been helping the inspector with his enquiries – that's it, isn't it?'

I exchanged glances with Virgilio. How come she knew that he was a police officer? She certainly didn't miss much.

I gave her the sort of look I used to give Oscar when he was younger and I found him drinking out of the toilet bowl. 'In spite of what you told me, I understand that you and Aldo were in a relationship after all.'

The beaming smile didn't leave her face for an instant. 'I wouldn't call it a relationship. We had an arrangement.'

Wow, I thought to myself, she really was a tough character. 'Aren't you sorry he's dead?'

Her expression became fractionally less happy. 'That rather depends on what happens now. I've been running this place for the last three years. I hope whoever inherits it realises that and understands how much I'm worth to the company.' She caught my eye. 'I don't suppose you happen to know who's going to inherit, do you? It's going to be complicated. I kept telling Aldo he needed to make a will, but he didn't listen.' Her tone became one of resignation. 'He never listened.'

I ignored her question and asked one of my own. 'Did you help him with the Etruscan antiquities racket?'

Her expression became one of blameless innocence. 'The police told me about that. I'm impressed. I didn't think he was that bright. It explains where he got his money from.'

'So you knew nothing about it?'

'Not a thing.' There was a twinkle in her eye as she carried on. 'If I'd known about it, I'm sure I could have helped him make a lot more money out of it than he did, but, like I said, he never mentioned it.'

In my years at Scotland Yard, I had only ever met a handful of people as adept at lying as Teresa. I found it hard to believe that she hadn't been in on the racket, but it was our word against hers, and she knew that we had no way of proving her involvement. Rather than bang my head against a brick wall, I changed the subject.

'So are you going to carry on running this place until the succession is finalised?'

'Why not? I already sign the cheques, pay suppliers and staff, and handle all the banking. Of course I'll carry on.' She smiled brightly again.

'I'll probably give myself a pay rise, though. I think that's only fair, don't you?'

Virgilio and I took Oscar up to the field and strolled up the track to the shed. Police tape now surrounded the whole building, and the front doors and the concealed rear door had been secured with padlocks to stop any more incursions. I wondered if the Etruscan treasures were still inside or if they had been moved. With Teresa now free and only just down the hill, I rather hoped that anything valuable had been removed. She was a formidable character and not the sort to be put off by a couple of padlocks.

23

THURSDAY EVENING

Signor Silvano's birthday party was a very smart affair. Signor Silvano himself turned up in a white tuxedo and all of the other staff were wearing their Sunday best. Rita was looking particularly glamourous in a striking red and blue gown and Elvis, the night porter, put in an appearance in an antique double-breasted dinner jacket that emanated such a strong smell of mothballs that Oscar dissolved into fits of sneezing every time he came close. The lounge had been decked with flowers and there was a terrific spread of nibbles on trays to one side. Antonio and Annamaria, the serving staff, came around with trays of champagne and we all toasted the octogenarian.

Rita gave a fine speech, outlining the history of the hotel, complimenting Signor Silvano on his business acumen and thanking him on behalf of all the staff for being a good and fair boss.

He replied with a few words, being very complimentary about everybody, particularly Rita, before being interrupted by a fit of coughing. After a couple of mouthfuls of champagne to calm the cough, he finished his brief speech and immediately went outside for a cigarette.

I left Anna talking history with Professor Scott of the University of London and wandered around the room, mainly following Oscar to make sure he didn't get too insistent with his begging for the tasty snacks. I chatted briefly to the chef, complimenting him on his prowess, and then found myself alongside Elvis.

I had only ever exchanged a handful of words with him, seeing as he came on duty late at night and went home very early in the morning, and I remembered Virgilio telling me that Inspector Fontana had said that his interview with him had produced nothing of interest. While Oscar positioned himself on the far side of me so as to be out of range of the mothballs, Elvis and I chatted a bit and I discovered that we shared a hobby – or at least he was fully invested in it, while I was very much a beginner. When I told him I'd been doing a windsurfing course, he launched into what was clearly his specialist subject and he was soon giving me valuable advice on the best way to gybe and water start. Considering that my final windsurfing session was going to be next day and I had pretty much given up all hope of performing either of these procedures, I listened with interest but knew that he was probably wasting his breath on me.

Things got a bit more interesting when he started talking about his childhood here in Santa Sabina. I finally managed to bring him around to the subject of the Graziani brothers, mentioning that I'd heard he used to work for Aldo at the campsite. A sour expression appeared on his face.

'I worked for Aldo's father for ten years and then for four years after his death while Aldo more than quadrupled the size of the campsite. I started the windsurfing academy and built that up for him. But then...' He took a mouthful of champagne but showed no sign of even tasting it.

I gave him a gentle nudge. 'But then...? Didn't things work out?'

He drained the last of the champagne in his glass and for a moment, I thought he might be about to dash it into the fireplace, but he restrained himself. 'But then he fired me.' His tone was bitter.

'After fourteen years, that must have hurt. Why did he fire you?' It occurred to me that Elvis might have been nurturing his resentment at being fired for four long years until it had suddenly erupted on Monday night. Might this good-looking young man be a murderer? It seemed highly unlikely that he would have waited so long, but I filed it away as another thread in this increasingly complex case.

'It was that woman, Teresa. She had a thing for me, and Aldo caught us kissing in one of the chalets... Well, a bit more than kissing, to be honest.

He threw a tantrum and fired me on the spot.' He looked up from his hands, straight into my eyes. 'But he didn't fire *her*.'

'And why do you think that was?'

'Why do you think? He was trying to get her into his bed, and, from what I've heard, he succeeded.' He caught my eye and winked ruefully. 'I doubt if she put up too much of a struggle.'

'So that's when you came to work here at the Augustus?'

He nodded. 'And I don't regret it one bit... Well, between you and me, there is one thing I regret.' I had to wait for him to continue but I concentrated my attention on Oscar and let Elvis take his time. When he finally spoke, it was in a stage whisper. 'Rita, she's my big regret.'

'You don't like Rita?'

'The opposite.' He took a surreptitious look around to check that he wasn't being overheard. 'We're the same age and she was my childhood sweetheart. I really thought we'd get married someday – and I thought she felt the same way. That's why I stayed on the island when she came back after university. I could have done a lot better for myself on the mainland but I wanted to be near her. Working at the campsite wasn't too bad. I only saw her now and then and it didn't hurt too bad, but working here means I see her every day and that's tough.'

'Tough because she doesn't share your feelings?'

I saw him nod glumly.

'Why do you think that is? Is there somebody else in her life?'

He shook his head ruefully. 'Nobody. It was all going fine until we were almost fifteen, and then she just switched off.'

'Switched off?'

'She lost all interest in me... or any other boy – and there were lots of them after her. As far as I can tell, she's been like it ever since.'

At that moment, Virgilio appeared at my elbow and led me outside so he could talk. There was a satisfied expression on his face – the same sort of expression that appears on Oscar's face when I give him bacon rinds.

'I've just taken a call from Piero. They found the murder weapon hidden in the bushes: a metal tube. You might be interested to hear that it's a piece of windsurfing equipment. There's blood on it and they've just got the results of the DNA testing and there's no doubt that the blood belongs to Aldo and the DNA at the other end of the weapon belongs to Fabio Morso. We've got him.'

I pumped his hand in triumph. There could be no doubt now. The murderer of Aldo Graziani had been caught. Of course, that still left the unanswered question of Ignazio.

We went back inside to give Anna and Lina the good news. By this time, Anna had stopped talking to the professor and was standing with Lina. I thought she was looking tired so I suggested we go and sit down. People were beginning to drift away by this time so the four of us went out onto the terrace and sat down at our usual table.

Rita appeared two minutes later with a tray of champagne and insisted that we help ourselves once more. In view of what Elvis had just told me, I took a closer look at her. She was definitely a good-looking woman and I wondered why she had turned her back on her paramour. It occurred to me that maybe, like Ingrid at the windsurfing school, she had discovered that she preferred members of her own sex, but that was none of my business and I made a deliberate attempt to get my mind onto less personal matters. I started by asking Lina what she wanted to do the next day – our last day here on the island – and she produced an interesting answer.

'Virgilio and I are going up Monte Capanne.'

'You're going mountain climbing?' Anna sounded appalled at the thought.

Lina giggled. 'You must be joking – it's over a thousand metres up. No, we're taking the cable car.'

Virgilio butted in. 'I keep telling you, it's not a cable car; it's a fairly primitive series of metal baskets attached to a cable. They only hold a couple of people each and they're exposed to the elements, so it's just as well we both have a good head for heights.' He glanced across at me and grinned. 'I don't think it would suit you, Dan.'

I shuddered theatrically. We all knew of my fear of heights. 'You're very welcome to your ride in the cable-car-metal-basket thing. Definitely not for me. And where is the mountain exactly?'

'Over in the west of the island. On a clear day, you can see mainland Italy in one direction and Corsica in the other direction. I'm really looking forward to it.' He glanced at Anna. 'What about you, Anna? I assume your boyfriend will be splashing about in the sea. Do you want to come with us?'

She shook her head. 'Thanks for the offer, but I'll be quite happy looking after Oscar while Dan does his thing out on the water.'

Ingrid had warned me that my final day of tuition was going to be concentrating on more advanced elements, so I had a feeling that I was going to be spending a lot of time in the water, rather than on it again. Still, I had to admit that I had enjoyed today. As long as I didn't drown tomorrow, that would be that.

After barely having had time for a quick sandwich at lunchtime – admittedly with a massive ice-cream sundae in the afternoon – I was feeling hungry so when dinnertime came, I opted for grilled sardines and squid rings as a starter, followed by ravioli filled with asparagus and mozzarella in a crab sauce. I was delighted to see Anna eating well and there was definitely more colour in her face today. Hopefully, her bandages would be removed in the next few days and she would soon regain full movement in her wounded shoulder. All in all, she had been very lucky, and I hoped that the judge would throw the book at Fabio Morso.

After dinner, I saw her back to the room and took Oscar for his evening stroll. While we walked about, my mind returned to the book I was writing and, for the first time in weeks, a glimmer of inspiration presented itself. The killer wasn't a man, but a woman. Up till now, I had been convinced that the murder had been committed by a man but, as I knew full well, murder is by no means the preserve of the male of the species. Of course she needed to have a powerful reason to see him dead, but what could that be? Suddenly, the thought of the alleged attempted abduction of a girl here at Santa Sabina flashed through my head and the answer came to me.

What if I borrowed that idea for my book? I could make it that years ago, the victim had assaulted and abused a young woman, ruining her life forever, and this murder was payback for that. I needed to work out how the two of them had met again and how it was he hadn't recognised her, but I felt a shot of excitement. I had found the solution to my dilemma and I now knew how to make the story work. I glanced down at Oscar, who was trotting happily beside me with a branch in his mouth.

'I've cracked it, Oscar. It was a woman and the death in San Gimignano was payback for something terrible that happened in the past.'

He looked back up at me, his eyes glowing green in the moonlight, and I swear he nodded.

Twenty minutes later, as I walked back along the clifftop path, I spotted a figure standing close to the cliff edge, staring out to the sea. Oscar trotted over to greet her and I saw that it was Rita.

'*Ciao*, Rita. It's a lovely night for a walk, isn't it?'

She turned towards us and the moonlight glistened against moisture on her cheeks. Had she been crying? When she answered, her voice was subdued. '*Ciao*, Dan.'

'Is everything all right? Signor Silvano's birthday party went well. I'm sure you organised the whole thing.' I tried to sound as cheerful as possible, although I was trying to work out what the trouble might be.

She mumbled a reply and returned her gaze to the sea. I could see she wanted to be on her own and I was about to wish her goodnight and turn away when I realised what had been staring me in the face for days. I'd been hoping that solving the murder of Ignazio Graziani might help me with my own book, and suddenly, I could see that it was the other way around. My book might just have provided the answer to the riddle of his death. We stood in silence for a minute or so while Oscar, instinctively sensing that Rita was upset, went over and leant against her leg in a show of support. Finally, keeping my voice as gentle and compassionate as possible, I brought the subject up.

'Can I ask you a personal question, Rita? How old are you?'

If she was surprised, she didn't show it. 'I'm thirty-five, almost thirty-six.'

'That's the same age as Elvis, isn't it?'

Again, there was just a deadpan reaction. 'He's two weeks older than me.'

I took a deep breath and said it. 'You're the girl that Ignazio tried to abduct twenty years ago, aren't you?'

Incredibly slowly, her head turned towards me and I could see the tears once more running down her cheeks. I had to wait almost a minute before she spoke, her voice low and husky. 'How did you know?'

'You told me you were at university on the mainland when it happened, but that was over twenty years ago so you would only have been fifteen. You were still here, weren't you?' She gave the faintest nod of the head and I went on. 'Tell me something: why didn't you go to the police about it?'

I had a long wait before she answered, but I didn't pressure her. When she finally spoke, her voice was clear, although her tone was subdued. 'It was my father mainly. He told me I'd brought shame on the family – as if it had been my fault. My mother was more sympathetic, but she agreed with him that it was best not to say anything, and, as far as everybody in the village was concerned, to act like nothing had happened.' I saw her eyes reach across the gap between us and her voice strengthened. 'How was I supposed to carry on as if nothing had happened after what he did to me?' Her voice almost cracked, but she rallied and continued. 'I don't know what you've heard, but it wasn't an attempted abduction. He pulled me into his van and he kept me in there with him for an hour: the longest hour of my life.' There was another pause before she carried on, her voice little more than a whisper. 'I was only fifteen and he raped me. How could I forget that?'

The pieces of the puzzle were falling into place, but I felt no sense of satisfaction. Up till now, I had believed that Ignazio's victims had been four. Now I knew that the true tally was five. I was pleased to see that Oscar was still staunchly at her side and her hand was gently stroking his head. All I felt was a deep sense of pity for her and revulsion at the behaviour of this man whose actions had caused so much pain to so many. I was going to say something, anything, to try to tell her that I understood, when she carried on talking in a studiously even voice.

'When I saw Ignazio again on Saturday night, I was determined to confront him. It was something I just knew I had to do. When my shift finished at ten o'clock, I didn't go home; I sneaked into the trees and watched him and his brother sitting at table with that woman, drinking and arguing. When Aldo and Teresa stormed off, I waited for my chance and it came when I saw Ignazio set off towards the cliff.' She rubbed the back of her hand across her cheeks but she didn't stop. 'I made my way around to head him off and you can imagine my surprise when I saw Virgilio come up the path from the beach and almost bump into Ignazio.

There was a scuffle and I saw Virgilio punch him so hard, he fell back into the trees only a few paces away from me.'

She paused and I had time to reflect that the presence Virgilio claimed to have sensed in the shadows had been his own cousin.

Before I could respond, Rita picked up the story again.

'Virgilio went off and after a bit, Ignazio pulled himself to his feet and wandered over here.' I saw her finger point at the ground right in front of her. 'It was here, in this exact same spot, that I came face to face with him. He stopped when he saw me, and I just stood there in silence, unable to say a word. As I looked at him, it all came back to me: the pain, the disgust and the shame.' She paused to take a few deep breaths. 'He stared at me blankly and mumbled, "Who are you?" He didn't recognise me. Can you imagine how that made me feel, Dan? Here he was, the man who had ruined my life, and he couldn't even remember my name.'

She lapsed into silence, and I could see from the movement of her shoulders that she was sobbing. My instincts were telling me to go over and give her a hug, but I didn't. I had to know what had happened.

Finally, after several minutes, I risked the all-important question.

'And so you pushed him over the cliff?'

She didn't look at me. She was staring down at her feet or maybe at Oscar, and I saw her shake her head slowly. 'I could have done, you know. I felt such a burning hatred inside me that I'm sure I could have pushed him, but I didn't. Instead, I just stood there in silence, staring at him in utter disgust.'

The detective in me told me that she would say this, wouldn't she, but I found myself believing her. I sensed she was too emotionally shaken to dissimulate, and when she continued, I could hear how hard she was struggling to keep control of her voice and her emotions.

'He was very drunk but he must have realised that I didn't want anything to do with him and he took two steps back and turned away. As he did so, I saw his foot slip and then, in the blink of an eye, he disappeared over the cliff edge. I didn't kill him. As it was, he did it all by himself. I'd like to think that he recognised me and did it deliberately as an act of contrition, but I know that isn't true. Animals like that don't go in for contrition.'

'Did you tell this to the police?' I already knew the answer, but I wanted to hear what she thought.

She shook her head. 'No, I knew how it would look so I said nothing, but I can't keep it to myself. I've hardly slept a wink since last Saturday. You're a good, fair man, and I'm sure you recognise the truth when you hear it. I needed to tell somebody, but not the police. I couldn't bear the thought of having it all raked up again. I knew it would be like going through it all over again. I thought I'd lose my mind.' She looked across at me and this time, her tone was almost matter-of-fact. 'That's why I decided to come out here now. It's the only way.'

She took a sideways step towards the edge of the cliff and I braced myself to rush forward and grab her, but Oscar at her side blocked her way. Keeping my eyes firmly on her, in case she made another move towards the edge, I stood there in silence for a while before the obvious course of action presented itself to me. Moving very slowly and deliberately so as not to startle her, I stepped towards her and took her gently by the arm, easing her away from the clifftop, and setting off in the direction of the hotel with Oscar still at her side. As we walked, I glanced towards her and I knew as I said it that I was doing the right thing.

'I'm not the police, Rita. Not now. As far as Ignazio's death's concerned, the case is closed. It's been decided that it was accidental death – just like you've just described it to me – and I see no reason to complicate things any more. I'm not going to say anything to anybody, not even Virgilio. That chapter of your history is closed and you have your whole life before you now.'

'Are you sure?' She raised her eyes towards me and I sensed a wave of relief running through her. 'I don't know how to thank you, Dan.'

'You don't need to thank me. It's over and he's gone. You did nothing wrong. Now's the time to make a fresh start and enjoy life to the full, but you don't need to do that on your own. Only this evening, I was talking to somebody who told me he loved you dearly. Why not take a chance and let him into your life? You know who I mean, don't you?'

She nodded in reply and a hint of a smile appeared on her face. 'I know.'

EPILOGUE
FRIDAY

My windsurfing session on Friday was as exhausting as I had expected, but I did it for Anna. Yes, on balance, I had to admit that I had enjoyed quite a lot of my week of windsurfing, but somehow, I didn't think I was going to go out and buy myself a board any time soon.

At the end of the afternoon, after splitting a bottle of Prosecco with Tatsuo, Ingrid and Stefano, I dragged Oscar away from this apparently limitless supply of tasty titbits, and Anna and I walked back along the coastal footpath towards the hotel. We let ourselves in through the gate in the fence and I led her to the top of the path above the private beach where we stopped to admire the view one last time. The beach itself was empty and the only sounds were a couple of noisy seagulls in the distance. The sea shimmered in the late-afternoon sun, a deep violet colour further out and the lightest of translucent blues by the shore. It was an idyllic spot – in spite of what had happened.

Feeling remarkably nervous, I set down my holdall and removed the little paper bag from the side pocket before turning towards Anna. I took her good hand in one of mine and leant forward to give her a gentle kiss.

She looked pleasantly surprised. 'What have I done to deserve that?'

'It would take me too long to tell you. Let's just say that you are you, and I love you for it.' I lowered myself onto one knee – ignoring the loud creak as I did so – opened the paper bag and pulled out the little box. I opened it and held it up towards her. 'Anna Galardo, will you marry me?'

Seeing me down at his level, Oscar wandered over to sniff the ring with interest, but I made sure I kept a good hold on it. The last thing I needed was for him to mistake it for a snack. I had the feeling that it might lose some of its romantic charm if it had to pass through my dog's alimentary canal before it could be retrieved.

Anna didn't answer at once, so I looked up hopefully.

'The lady in the shop said that if you didn't like it, she'd be happy to exchange it, and if you said no, she'd give me my money back. You will say yes, won't you?'

She still didn't reply immediately, and an awful feeling of dread began to descend on me, but finally, she reached down and caught hold of my free hand, squeezing it tightly. At first, I was shocked to see tears glistening in her eyes, but she soon put my fears to rest, and an immense feeling of relief spread through me.

'Of course I will. There's nothing I'd like more. I thought you'd never ask.'

Sensing the emotion in the air, Oscar nudged me with his nose and set about licking my ear. I patted his nose and then stood back up again, stepping towards Anna.

'You do realise that you won't just be marrying me.' I shot an affectionate glance down at Oscar, who was standing at my side, tail wagging slowly. 'Love me, love my dog.'

She grinned at me. 'I wouldn't want it any other way.'

* * *

MORE FROM T. A. WILLIAMS

In case you missed it, the previous instalment in the Armstrong and Oscar cozy mystery series from T. A. Williams, *Murder at the Ponte Vecchio*, is available to order now here:

https://mybook.to/PonteVecchioBackAd

ACKNOWLEDGEMENTS

Warmest thanks to Emily Ruston, my lovely editor at the marvellous Boldwood Books, as well as the rest of the Boldwood team. Sincere thanks also to Sue Smith and Emily Reader for picking up all my errors and making sure that everything makes sense. Special thanks to the talented Simon Mattacks for narrating the audio versions of all the books in the Dan and Oscar series. To me, he sounds just like Dan should sound. Finally, thanks to Mariangela, my wife, whose family introduced me to the island of Elba years ago. If you haven't been there, I do recommend it highly.

ABOUT THE AUTHOR

T. A. Williams is the author of The Armstrong and Oscar Cozy Mystery Series, cosy crime stories set in his beloved Italy, featuring the adventures of DCI Armstrong and his labrador Oscar. Trevor lives in Devon with his Italian wife.

Sign up to T. A. Williams' newsletter to read an EXCLUSIVE short story!

Visit T. A. Williams' website: www.tawilliamsbooks.com

Follow T. A. Williams' on social media:

facebook.com/TrevorWilliamsBooks

x.com/TAWilliamsBooks

bsky.app/profile/tawilliamsbooks.bsky.social

ALSO BY T. A. WILLIAMS

The Armstrong and Oscar Cozy Mystery Series

Murder in Tuscany

Murder in Chianti

Murder in Florence

Murder in Siena

Murder at the Matterhorn

Murder at the Leaning Tower

Murder on the Italian Riviera

Murder in Portofino

Murder in Verona

Murder in the Tuscan Hills

Murder at the Ponte Vecchio

Murder on an Italian Island

Poison
& Pens

POISON & PENS IS THE HOME OF
COZY MYSTERIES SO POUR YOURSELF
A CUP OF TEA & GET SLEUTHING!

DISCOVER PAGE-TURNING NOVELS FROM
YOUR FAVOURITE AUTHORS &
MEET NEW FRIENDS

JOIN OUR
FACEBOOK GROUP

BIT.LYPOISONANDPENSFB

SIGN UP TO OUR
NEWSLETTER

BIT.LY/POISONANDPENSNEWS

Boldwood

Boldwood Books is an award-winning fiction publishing company seeking out the best stories from around the world.

Find out more at www.boldwoodbooks.com

Join our reader community for brilliant books, competitions and offers!

Follow us
@BoldwoodBooks
@TheBoldBookClub

Sign up to our weekly deals newsletter

https://bit.ly/BoldwoodBNewsletter

www.ingramcontent.com/pod-product-compliance
Ingram Content Group UK Ltd.
Pitfield, Milton Keynes, MK11 3LW, UK
UKHW040815230725
7005UKWH00011B/13

9 781835 188019